Afterdark

The Midnight Museum

Also by Annie Dalton

The first two books in the Afterdark series
The Afterdark Princess
The Dream Snatcher

Night Maze
Out of the Ordinary
Naming the Dark

For younger readers

Space Baby
The Real Tilly Beany
Tilly Beany and the Best Friend Machine
Tilly Beany Saves the World

Tyler Rapido adventures
Tyler and the Talk Stalk
Dozy Rosy
The Frog Files
Jam Jar Genie

Afterdark

The Midnight Museum

ANNIE DALTON

Mammoth

First published in Great Britain 2001 by Mammoth
an imprint of Egmont Children's Books
a division of Egmont Holding Limited
239 Kensington High Street, London W8 6SA

Text copyright © 2001 Annie Dalton
Cover illustration copyright © 2001 Paul Hess

The moral rights of the author and cover illustrator have been asserted

ISBN 0 7497 4624 6

4 6 8 10 9 7 5

A CIP catalogue record for this title is available from the British Library

Typeset by Avon DataSet Ltd, Bidford on Avon, Warwickshire
Printed in Great Britain by
Cox & Wyman Ltd, Reading, Berkshire

for Maria
with heartfelt thanks
A. D.

Contents

1
Joe's warning

As Joe Quail hurtled downstairs on the first day of term, he noticed a strange envelope on the doormat.

He knew it wasn't a regular letter. For one thing, there was no stamp. For another, it had the faintest gleam of moonlight.

Scrawled across the front was an ominous message:

A warning to Joe Quail.

Joe tore open the envelope and slid out a piece of torn crackly paper. The writing was old-fashioned and flowery, making it hard to read.

'*And darkness will rule*,' he read slowly.

Joe was no stranger to magical happenings, but it was the first time he'd received an ancient curse through his letterbox. The shock made him so wobbly that he had to sit down. To his astonishment, the writing vanished and new words shimmered in their place.

'*And light will shine,*' he now read, bewildered.

He tipped the sheet of paper experimentally. The first message returned. Relief surged through him. 'Nice try, Kevin,' he grinned.

In this world, Kevin Kitchener was just another tough kid. But in the world of Afterdark, where he and Joe first became friends, Kevin was a warrior and a hero. He was also a wicked practical joker.

Kevin had been away all summer, staying with his sister. Presumably scaring Joe half to death with a curse was Kevin's way of saying he was back in town.

Joe hovered outside the kitchen, plucking up courage to go in. It sounded suspiciously quiet and he needed to figure out if it was a friendly family-type silence, or the stomach-churning kind.

For as long as Joe could remember, there had just been him and his mum. Then over the summer holidays he'd acquired a new dad, two stepsisters and a small black cat called Betty Einstein. Now they lived all cooped up together in one tiny terraced house, and the strain was starting to show.

As it happened, Joe totally approved of his new family. He thought his stepdad, Tom, was really good news, and he secretly adored the cat. He was also quite fond of his sisters. There was just one small complication.

They were not entirely human.

Technically, Flora and Titania (Tat for short), were only half-vampire.

It was their mother who had been a true vampire, though not, as Flora kept reminding Joe, the horror-film kind; so neither sister showed the slightest interest in human blood. Flora fainted at the sight of it, though little Tat could give you a nasty nip if you weren't careful.

But having vampire ancestors wasn't exactly something Flora wanted to get out. Even her own dad didn't know the truth. So after their parents' wedding, she'd made Joe swear a solemn vow to keep their magic lives and their real lives separate.

'Mum said mixing them up just leads to big trouble,' she said sternly.

'I'll feel like a double agent,' Joe complained.

Flora gave him a crooked little smile. 'Join the club.'

Leading a double life turned out to be incredibly hard work. It seemed that once you started acquiring secrets, you couldn't stop. Without intending to, Joe was becoming a kind of secrets magnet. Some of them were fairly tame, like where Joe's mum had hidden his stepdad's birthday present. Others, like the vampire thing, were pure dynamite.

Not only did Joe live in terror of letting something slip, he was also constantly having to make tricky decisions at the drop of a hat.

For instance, should he tell Flora about his joke

warning, or not? Probably not, he decided. She'd been up since dawn, ironing non-existent creases out of her school blouse and double-checking the contents of her shiny new school briefcase. Starting high school was clearly a big deal for Flora. For some reason it hadn't quite sunk in with Joe yet.

He checked his expression in the hall mirror. Drop the guilty grin, he told himself. It's a dead giveaway. Try to look like someone with a totally clear conscience. *That's* more like it!

He took a deep breath and flung open the kitchen door. Wow, he thought.

It looked exactly like a breakfast food commercial! Sunlight was pouring through the window, giving everyone soft sunshiney halos. His family looked so perfect he could have cried.

Ideally, Flora would have been eating her cereal, instead of picking out the freeze-dried raspberries and frowning at her book of Advanced Brainteasers. Also Joe's stepdad would have waited till *after* breakfast before sorting through the bills.

But for those precious sunlit moments, Flora was not an irritable vampire child with bizarre eating habits. She was a quirky girl genius. And little Tat was not planning her next act of evil sabotage, but just humming innocently in her highchair. And then the sun went in.

Joe's dad tossed the bills aside. 'And they all lived happily ever after,' he said grimly. 'In jail.'

Joe's mum didn't seem to hear. She was reading the house ads in the local paper. 'Tom!' she said excitedly. 'This one's got two bathrooms and an attic, which would be ideal for your study.'

'Ideal for a millionaire,' he growled.

'No, listen!' But she'd only read as far as the luxurious master-bathroom, when Tat gave an ear-splitting shriek, and hurled her bowl across the kitchen.

'Ouf!' said Joe, amazed to find himself dripping with porridge.

All at once everybody was yelling at everybody else.

'You were supposed to be watching her!' yelled Joe's mum. 'That child is a demon!'

'You distracted me with your outrageous gold fireplaces and marble taps!' Joe's dad yelled back.

'Stop it, both of you!' screamed Flora. 'I'm going to a scary new high school in exactly ten minutes and twenty-five seconds. I don't need any more STRESS!' And she rushed out.

'Excellent,' Joe muttered. 'I get the porridge and *she's* stressed.'

His mum quickly mopped him down with some kitchen towel. 'Better check if Flora's OK,' she said guiltily.

Once upon a time, Joe was a lonely only. Now, as well as

being a secrets magnet, he was everyone's favourite go-between. He found his sister huddled at the bottom of the stairs, tensely studying her book.

'Erm. I wouldn't read too much into that demon thing,' he said. 'Mum has no idea about your vampire DNA, honestly.'

'GO AWAY,' said Flora stonily.

So much for sympathy, thought Joe. OK, we'll try wacky.

He put on his school blazer. His hands immediately disappeared from view. He flapped his empty sleeves. 'I don't know why you're worried,' he said. 'Your uniform fits. I look like some little elf. Can you believe this was the smallest size they had?'

'Shut UP, Joe,' she growled.

He sat down beside her. 'I've got a maths problem for you.'

His sister rolled her eyes.

'I'm serious. What are the odds of our house being struck by a meteorite in the next eight minutes, putting an end to life as we know it?'

Flora's face crumpled. 'Didn't that just happen!' A tear splashed on her shoe. 'Everything feels so weird, Joe,' she choked. 'Home. School. It's like my whole world changed overnight.'

In Joe's opinion, Flora needed serious cheering up. So just this once, he broke the rules. 'You mean this world,' he said softly. 'Not Afterdark and not Alice. They'll never ever change.'

Of all Joe's many secrets, the wildest and most wonderful had to be Alice Fazackerly. To adults she was just the perfect teenage babysitter; calm, sensible and perfectly reliable. But her true identity was far more mysterious.

Flora smiled a watery little smile. 'Yeah,' she whispered. 'How many kids have a magic princess for a babysitter?'

Yess! thought Joe. His ruse had worked! 'She's coming tomorrow,' he reminded her. 'I can't wait, can you?'

But the moment had passed. Flora sniffed back her tears. 'Help!' she said in her normal voice. 'What did I do with that stupid compass?'

It had finally arrived, the moment Joe had been dreading. He'd always known he'd go to the high school one day. He'd just hoped to be three inches taller by the time that day came.

As they reached the gates, he froze in panic. 'I can't go in there! Have you seen the size of those boys? They'll murder me.'

Flora pulled a face. 'And all the girls will hate me like poison. They always do.' Her expression softened. 'You'll be OK. The main thing is not to react and eventually they'll get bored. Oh, well, good luck.' She ploughed bravely into the crowd.

Joe wished all these big scary thugs would stop playing football, so he could scout around for Kevin. Then it dawned on him. Kevin was the big scary thug with the ball! Kevin had grown huge since Joe saw him last. He'd also acquired a ferocious new haircut, which made him look practically bald. But apart from his height and his hair, Kevin was exactly the same as ever.

'Joe Quail, my man,' he yelled, delighted. He casually headed the ball to another kid and loped across, grinning his famous shark's grin.

'Nice curse,' said Joe at once. 'Really had me going. The paper looked ancient. Did you use coffee, or just stick it in the gas burner?'

Kevin looked blank. 'Sorry, mate. I have no idea what you're on about.'

Joe felt a twinge of panic. 'I thought you sent it as a joke.'

Kevin shook his head. 'Ancient curses aren't my style. I'm a whoopee cushion kind of guy. Sounds more like Vasco to me.'

'I never thought of him,' said Joe.

Vasco Shine was a distant relation of Flora's. When the children first met him, he was a young, smooth-talking villain. These days, in daylight hours at least, Vasco ran a hot-air balloon business called Dream Catchers. But there was always that tiny whiff of danger about him. Flora said that's why all the girls fancied him.

Just then the school bell went, leaving Joe's question unanswered.

To his relief he'd been put in the same class as Flora and Kevin.

They spent the first lesson copying down the class timetable. In the second lesson, they rubbed the first timetable out again and copied down the correct timetable. 'Yahoo, it's Groundhog Day!' whispered Kevin. 'If they keep this up, we'll never do any lessons at all!'

The boy at the next desk wore a huge hooded coat. He glowered out from under his outsize hood like a gangster and Joe felt a dangerous tension leaking from him like static electricity. This kid couldn't sit still for an instant. Every time the teacher said anything, he rolled his eyes and gave an exasperated sigh. Joe got the impression that his twitchy neighbour was ready to kick over his chair and storm out, if things didn't improve.

The teacher, whose name Joe couldn't seem to catch, handed round exercise books. The boy in the hood immediately scrawled the word 'Spoon' across his, in huge uneven letters. He glanced up and caught Joe looking. 'What's your problem, shorty?' he snarled. Spoon had strange staring eyes, which made him look perpetually furious about something.

'No, nothing,' stuttered Joe.

'Yeah, right,' said the boy contemptuously.

Some of the other boys sniggered.

Kevin gave Joe a nudge. 'Don't mind him. Spoon's a bit of a maniac, but he's a laugh when you get to know him.'

But Joe somehow couldn't quite picture becoming buddies with Spoon.

He was faintly miffed to see Flora chatting to one of the girls. None of the girls at their old school ever had anything to do with her. 'They think I'm weird,' Flora had explained gloomily. 'They just don't know *how* weird.'

At break, she came over, pink with excitement. 'Have you heard? There's this peculiar illness going around.'

'Excellent,' said Kevin at once. 'I can stay at home and watch loads of MTV.'

'You don't want this one,' Flora told him. 'The kids who've got it fall into a sleeping beauty-type sleep and can't wake up.'

Kevin snorted. 'Yeah right, and then rose petals like, gracefully flutter down and cover them.'

'Are you sure it's not just some seniors trying to freak out the first-years?' suggested Joe.

Flora looked embarrassed. 'Now you mention it, it *is* only first-years that are meant to be affected.'

'And you fell for it?' said Kevin.

She shrugged. 'What can I say, Kev? I'm a girl.'

As the children walked home after school, a girl waved to

them. She had swingy black hair and the most angelic face Joe had ever seen.

'Oh hiya!' called Flora.

'Oh *hiya*,' said Kevin under his breath.

'Who's that?' demanded Joe.

Flora seemed maddeningly serene. 'Don't yell,' she said. 'Her name's Clare Ying. She's in my maths group, and she's an Afterdark kid like us. Isn't that amazing?'

'You talked to her about Alice?' Joe was appalled.

'I had a hunch, OK? The moment I saw her, I had this funny feeling, as if I knew her already. Then when we were getting changed for PE, I noticed she'd got this weird burn-mark on her arm. It looks exactly like a dream-burn,' Flora explained. 'The kind you get in the dream fields, when a dream blasts off without warning and you're standing too close. So I asked her about it, and it turned out I was right.'

Kevin whistled. 'You took a risk!'

'I told you, I had a hunch. Anyway, she's a really nice person.'

'Yeah,' agreed Kevin thoughtfully. 'She looks all right.'

Joe's first day at his new school also turned out to be his best.

After that it was downhill all the way. The teachers spoke in Martian. The kids were mean. But worst of all, wherever

Joe went, there was Spoon, eyes blazing, asking him what his problem was.

'Don't take it so personally,' Kevin kept saying.

It was all right for him. Smaller kids had always thought Kevin was cool. And the bigger kids would never dream of picking on him. But Joe couldn't even escape into the toilets for a rest. The second-years hurled water bombs or soggy toilet paper at any first-years venturing into their territory.

Then Tuesday night came at last, and all Joe's worries disappeared, except for one. But though he distinctly heard Tat sneeze several times during tea, neither parent even mentioned cancelling their night out.

Minutes before Alice was due to arrive, Joe and Flora were in the front room, watching the street.

Joe heard his parents coming downstairs. 'She's cutting it fine,' murmured Tom.

'The clock must be fast,' joked his mum. 'Alice has to be the most reliable teenager on this planet.'

But the clock ticked on. Suddenly the phone rang.

Flora and Joe exchanged stricken looks. 'That's not Alice,' said Joe fiercely. 'She'd never just phone.'

Joe's mum popped her head around the door. 'Bad news,' she said. 'Some family emergency. I must say,' she added crossly, 'I do think Alice could have told us earlier.'

Without a word, Joe walked upstairs and shut himself in

his room. He felt numb. Alice never let them down. It was like one of those cosmic laws Flora went on about.

Now Joe felt as if he didn't even know her. He'd had no idea Alice even had a family. She rarely talked about herself and Joe never thought to ask. It never seemed to matter. Until now.

Hours later, Flora crept in. 'Are you awake?' she whispered.

'Unless I'm dreaming this conversation.'

'Oh ha ha.' His sister perched beside him in the dark.

'I thought we were so special,' he said miserably.

'Oh, do grow up,' she snapped. 'In all this time, Alice has let you down once! Didn't it occur to you she might have a good reason?'

Joe wasn't listening. 'Now suddenly there's all these other Afterdark kids we didn't know about. We don't even know where Alice lives. I mean does she actually have a home? What if she's just decided to dump us and we never see her again?'

'Will you listen! You heard your mum. Alice had a family emergency!'

Joe felt a thrill of fear. 'You mean her Afterdark family!' He sat up. 'What do you think's happened?'

'Something big,' said Flora tersely. 'We'll call in at Dream Catchers on the way to school. Vasco will know what's going on.'

'I thought you said to keep everything separate,' Joe

reminded her. 'You know, magic and real life don't mix, blah blah blah.'

Flora had an annoying habit of mumbling insults so you couldn't answer back. She did it now, growling something that sounded like, 'Worra worra worra', and stalked out, leaving Joe feeling vaguely on edge.

But when Joe and Flora turned up at Dream Catchers next day, they received a terrible shock. The sign, with its familiar balloon logo, had been replaced by a TO LET notice. Not a trace of Vasco's business remained.

'It's like we just dreamed it,' whispered Joe.

Flora clenched her fists. 'This gets worse and worse.'

'You don't think Vasco's, you know, gone back to his old ways?' asked Joe anxiously.

'You're just saying that because he's a vampire,' she snapped.

Joe sighed. 'No, I'm saying that because he's Vasco, you dummy.'

After school, Flora had chess club and Kevin stayed for football practice. After his dismal performance at games earlier that day, Joe didn't see the point of trying out. He trudged home alone, feeling like a complete loser.

He turned into his street and saw someone jogging towards him; a cheerful freckled youth, humming to his personal stereo.

But as they drew level, an eerie change came over the

jogger. His eyes swivelled emptily in Joe's direction. '*And darkness will rule,*' he said in a toneless voice. Then he looked dazed and jogged away.

Joe stood stock-still in the middle of the street.

That didn't happen, he told himself; but all at once he couldn't breathe.

Evil had come too close. A normal human being had changed inexplicably into a zombie, and for a terrifying instant something had looked out at Joe and uttered a chilling warning from another world.

Suddenly he saw zombies everywhere. The couple with the silly little dog. The old ladies in the launderette.

'Darkness will rule,' Joe whispered. '*Darkness will rule . . .*'

He took off down the street and didn't stop running until he reached home. He let himself in and leaned on the door, breathing in great tearing gasps.

A dark magic was leaking into their world, and only one person could tell him why. Alice, the Afterdark princess.

They *had* to find her. But how?

2
A deep and deadly sleep

Tom came out of the kitchen while Joe was getting his breath back.

'I thought I heard you,' he said. 'Could you watch Tat, while I pop out to the supermarket?'

'Sure,' Joe managed to croak.

Tom grabbed his battered leather jacket and checked for his keys.

'Maybe you should keep a look out for Flora on the way,' said Joe casually. 'I heard there's some nutter hanging around.' What else could he say? Beware of the zombies?

Tom ruffled his hair. 'You two are good mates, aren't you?' he said, as if this still surprised him. And he was gone.

It seemed like hours until Joe heard Tom's key in the door. Flora and Kevin were with him.

'Is it me, or is there a weird atmosphere out there?' Tom was saying.

Flora rolled her eyes. 'Honestly, you writers!'

'Yeah, you live in another world,' said Kevin in the same false jokey voice.

Joe didn't have to ask if they'd seen the zombies.

'We're going up to my room, Dad, OK?' said Flora.

As soon as they were upstairs, she shut her door.

'Mum was right,' she said shakily. 'When the real and magic worlds get mixed up, it leads to big BIG trouble.'

She went to the window and peered out. Nothing moved, except for the pigeons waddling around on next door's roof. Flora yanked down her blind. 'You never know,' she shivered. 'He might be nobbling pigeons too.'

'How do you know it's a he?' asked Joe.

Flora glared. 'He, she, *it*. Sorry, Joe. What do you call a powerful magic being who sends kids evil zombie-grams?'

'Don't pick on Joe!' said Kevin mildly. 'He sent your dad to get you, remember!'

'Are you OK, Kev?' asked Joe. 'You look terrible.'

Kevin forced a grin. 'I don't mind something I can take a good whack at,' he explained. 'But those people were like his innocent transmitters or something.'

Flora suddenly looked sick. 'What if he turns Betty Einstein into some kind of creepy zombie cat?'

Joe grinned. 'Nah! You've got to have at least one brain cell to qualify for a zombie.'

Flora gave an edgy little giggle. 'That's so mean. Betty's mad about you.' Her smile faded and she peered around the corner of her blind. 'I *hate* this!' she fumed. 'It's like being on closed circuit TV. Any time it wants, it can switch on a passing stranger and see what we're up to.'

'But why would anyone *do* that?' asked Joe.

'It wants to freak us out,' said Kevin. 'It can't get into our world, so it's doing it from a distance.'

Joe was horrified. 'You think it's controlling people from Afterdark? Is that possible?'

'Not normally,' said Flora.

Joe shook his head. 'Boy, we really need Alice.'

'Maybe Clare knows where we could find her?' suggested Kevin.

Joe was wildly jealous at the idea that Flora's new friend might have privileged information about Alice. But it turned out that Clare was a relative newcomer to Afterdark.

'Alice only started babysitting for Clare's family a couple of months ago, so she's just as much in the dark as we are,' said Flora bleakly. 'Clare says, when her family want a sitter, they leave messages at Alice's school.'

Suddenly Kevin's face lit up. 'We're pathetic! The sixth form college is just across the road from our school! We'll meet her out of school. Then she'll *have* to tell us what's going on.'

Flora looked uneasy. 'Maybe Alice doesn't want us mixed up in this.'

'Tough,' snarled Kevin. 'What if she's in danger? What if she's in mortal danger and she needs *us*?'

Joe felt ashamed. He hadn't thought of that. 'Tell you what, we'll hide,' he said. 'And when Alice comes out of school, we'll follow her.'

Flora pulled a face. 'That seems so sneaky.'

'Yeah?' Kevin tapped his stubbly skull. 'Well sometimes, my girl, you've got to use a bit of this.'

Next day the children waited anxiously as teenagers streamed out through the gates of Alice's school. Joe felt sick with nerves. What if Alice wasn't there? Or what if she was, but she didn't want anything more to do with them?

Then he saw her coming through the crowd and his doubts melted away. With her clear grey eyes and shining hair, Alice was every bit as dear and beautiful as ever.

'Sorry,' Joe heard her say in a firm voice. 'I can't come tonight.'

In a few brisk steps Alice crossed the street, leaving her friends behind.

The children trailed her across town, dodging between parked cars and crouching behind phone boxes. She was heading for the oldest part of town, down by the river. Then, in a rundown street full of abandoned cars and lock-up garages, she gave them the slip.

'How did *that* happen?' moaned Joe.

Flora went scouting ahead and came back beaming. 'It's not a dead-end after all. It's an alley.'

And at the end of the secret alley was a building so ancient that they could only stare.

'It looks like it just grew,' whispered Kevin. 'Bits sprouting everywhere.'

'There's a tower,' breathed Flora.

'Trust Alice to have a tower,' said Kevin.

'If this is actually where she lives,' said Joe cautiously.

Flora peeled back strands of ivy, revealing a battered sign. 'Look!'

'The Midnight Museum,' Joe read aloud. His skin prickled all over at the words.

They walked around the museum, trying doors without success. Joe could hear a bird on some distant rooftop, singing over and over.

Eventually they found themselves in a sunny courtyard. In front of them was a door. On either side of it, someone had planted strange flowers the size of hollyhocks. Their silky blooms were the colour of summer moonlight.

Joe sniffed one. It smelled like Alice.

'Evening primroses,' said Flora softly. 'They only flower at night.'

'She lives here all right,' said Kevin.

Flora tried the courtyard door, but it too remained stubbornly closed. 'You try, Joe.'

Joe jiggled the latch. 'Let us in,' he pleaded. 'We've come to see Alice.'

The sound was so faint, Joe wasn't sure if he'd imagined the starry, faraway chimes. But the latch gave way under his hand.

Kevin gave them a dreamy smile. 'Don't you love magic?'

Flora seemed wary. 'Sometimes.'

The children went inside.

The ground floor was a bit of a let-down, just dusty boxes piled from floor to ceiling. Beyond the boxes was a staircase with fraying rope for a bannister. Kevin went pounding up to the top. 'No sign of Alice,' he called. 'But I've found the museum. It's kind of weird.'

Flora and Joe tore upstairs to join him and found themselves in a long, low space filled with dusty showcases.

Some of the exhibits seemed left over from a magical fairytale. Others were as dark and eerie as Joe's dreams.

Kevin was scowling at a tall stringed instrument. 'Forget what I said about magic. What kind of creep comes up with something like this?'

Joe peered at the label. 'The Nightingale Harp,' he read aloud.

Flora covered her ears. 'Don't tell me!' She fled out of earshot.

'It won't be made out of actual little birdie bones,' Joe said hastily. 'It just means it *sounds* really incredible.'

'Look closer,' said Kevin darkly. 'You can see the joins.'

Joe swallowed. 'No thanks, Kev.'

He went to look for Flora. She was gazing intently at some ancient jewellery, mesmerised by a small, darkly-glittering stone. Joe thought it looked like an egg laid by a rather sinister bird.

Her expression was unusually soft. 'Isn't it lovely? It's a storm-stone. Mum had one just like it.'

Joe stared at it obligingly, trying to see what she saw. 'Sorry, Flo. Must be a vampire thing.'

Flora gave him a sour grin. 'Yeah. Must be.'

'There has to be another staircase somewhere,' said Kevin.

A breeze went whispering across the museum, lifting the corner of a faded tapestry. Behind it was a second flight of stairs, one so narrow and winding that as he climbed, Joe banged his elbows at every step.

And on the highest stair, not in the least surprised to see them, was Alice. 'Come in,' she said.

They followed her into a sunny room, overlooking the river. A large mirror sent watery reflections rippling across the walls.

Alice's schoolbooks were spilled across a table, mixed up with Afterdark books with titles like *The Secret Wisdom of Trolls*, and the *A–Z of Sorcery*. She hastily folded up what seemed to be a very old map. 'Excuse the mess. I've got exams. In both worlds, worse luck.'

'We had to come,' said Joe apologetically.

'I'd have been disappointed if you hadn't,' she said.

Flora sounded edgy. 'You make it sound like a test!'

Alice shook her head. 'Not a test exactly. But I needed to be sure.'

'I don't get you,' said Kevin.

Alice sighed. 'I'm afraid this isn't going to be like our other times.'

'What do you mean?' asked Joe in alarm.

Flora looked as if she might burst into tears. 'Could you just tell us what's going on? When you didn't turn up, we went to see Vasco. And he's *gone*.'

'We didn't know if he'd done a runner, or if that — that zombie thing got him,' said Kevin.

Instead of answering, Alice walked across to the mirror. 'This must all seem very strange and frightening. You have a right to know what's going on. But first there are some people who need to talk to you.'

The children stared at her.

'Which people?' asked Kevin suspiciously.

'It won't take long. They're expecting you.' Alice touched her hand lightly to the mirror. The glass became dazzlingly fluid and together Alice and the three children passed through it as effortlessly as air.

Joe found himself in a vast candle-lit hall, surrounded by people in stiff black and silver clothes. For a second, he felt as if he'd been set down on a giant chessboard. Then the figures sprang to life.

A dignified old man in robes beckoned to them. 'Welcome,' he called. 'Warm yourselves by the fire.'

'Come and meet my grandparents,' said Alice. 'The king and queen of Afterdark.'

Joe was horrified. What was Alice thinking of, dragging them off to meet magical royalty without so much as a warning? It was all right for her. With her wild hair tumbling down her back, Alice looked every inch a magical princess. But Joe and Flora still wore their hideous school uniform. As usual, Kevin was wearing his own personal uniform of tracksuit and trainers.

Joe nervously shook hands with the elderly king and queen. The queen was stooped and frail, but when she smiled, Joe saw that she had Alice's sparkling grey eyes.

Looking strangely out of place amongst the lords and ladies were dozens of Afterdark warriors, their uniforms bright against the wintry colours of the court.

Flora pulled a face. 'Ugh! I just saw a troll general.'

'It's a council of war, bird-brain,' said Kevin. 'They have to invite all the generals, don't they!'

The children were given places of honour at the grand table.

The king came straight to the point. 'Danger threatens both our worlds. Danger which was foretold long ago in the book of prophecy.'

Kevin looked horribly embarrassed. 'Oh, please,' he muttered.

Flora kicked him hard. 'Behave!'

But Joe felt a thrill of fear.

'Today, we meet under one roof,' the king continued. 'Loyal friends and ancient enemies, magicians and warriors, Midnights and Shines, to fight our common foe.'

'Shines,' blurted Joe. 'Vasco's family, you mean?'

The king frowned. 'Vasco has given us trouble in the past,' he said sternly. 'But we were forced to revise our opinion. He has recently earned our gratitude by volunteering for a dangerous mission.'

Kevin perked up. 'He's gone into deep cover, hasn't he?'

The king looked startled. 'Indeed,' he said. 'If by that, you mean all traces of his existence in your world were erased.'

'It worked,' said Kevin. 'It totally did our heads in.'

'My dear, we have so little time,' murmured the queen. 'Why don't you show them the book.'

A very small boy stepped forward, clutching an enormous leather-bound book.

Alice gave them a mischievous smile. 'Sorry, Kevin. There really is an old prophecy. And you're in it. Actually, you're all in it.'

She held the book so it was facing them, and opened the cover.

Its brittle pages glowed with magical colours. In the margins were fabulous beasts and magical trees.

Suddenly, Joe was sure he'd seen this handwriting before. Someone had posted a fragment of this strange book through Joe's letterbox. He was almost certain it was Vasco. But why?

Alice turned a page. 'And here you all are.'

Flora gasped. 'They even got your smile, Kevin.'

Kevin struggled to look unimpressed. 'So basically, this says we save the day, right?'

Alice smiled. 'Only time will show that.'

'It does say you children are our only hope,' said the queen.

Flora examined the writing closely. 'Excuse me, your majesties. What does this part mean?' She cleared her throat nervously. 'By winning they will lose. By losing they will win.'

'Interesting you should mention that, my dear,' said the king. 'These words have caused great confusion amongst Afterdark scholars.' He sighed. 'It rather makes you wonder if writers of prophecies simply enjoy being mysterious.'

Joe was still gazing yearningly at their picture in the book of prophecy. These were the superstar versions of Joe, Kevin and Flora, more glorious in every way than their real life selves. Fabulous heroes in some fairytale yet to be written; cool, tough and completely unbeatable.

Once Joe had been afraid of everything. Water, heights, other children. After he met Alice, it seemed he'd conquered his childish fears for ever. Then, to his shame, they'd sprung up again like weeds, as if he'd just been kidding himself he'd got the better of them. As if he'd have to spend his whole life hacking them down again and again.

From somewhere far away, Joe heard the king say, 'It will mean going into certain danger.'

Danger! The word jumped out at him. Was that what he needed?

If Joe faced this new terror and fulfilled the prophecy, would he be a true hero at last, like that boy in the book?

He swallowed hard and heard himself say, 'I think the danger already came to us, your majesty. I'd be honoured to help.'

'Yeah, count me in,' Kevin agreed.

Flora nodded. 'And me.'

And they were back on the right side of the mirror, in the rippling river-light.

They should have been home ages ago, but Joe was reluctant to leave.

Here, in Alice's calm little apartment between the worlds, amongst her books of high magic, it seemed quite natural to be a superstar hero.

He hung about at the top of the stairs. 'You're worried, aren't you?' he asked shyly. 'About Vasco.'

'Yes,' said Alice. 'Yes, I am.'

Flora yanked at his sleeve. 'Come on. Alice has got stuff to do. Don't see us out, Alice. We know the way.'

'Yeah,' grinned Kevin. 'Back to that old grindstone, girl!'

On their way out, they somehow managed to lose Flora. She caught them up in the courtyard. 'Sorry. Stone in my shoe!' she panted.

Kevin gave her a searching look. 'Are you OK?'

Flora frowned. 'Why wouldn't I be?'

'You just look a bit hot and bothered.'

'Thanks a bunch,' she sniffed. 'Now can we just go home, please?'

And Joe's sister went stomping off; as if they'd been keeping her waiting, he thought, and not the other way around.

It wasn't a lie. She did have a stone in her shoe.

Flora hadn't known where else to put it. The instant they got home, she mumbled an excuse, and bolted to her room.

Betty Einstein was dozing on Flora's bed, where she was strictly forbidden to be. She opened a wary yellow eye. When she saw it was only Flora, she yawned, stretching out a friendly paw.

Flora was in such a hurry, she couldn't even wait to untie her shoe. She just tore it off, its laces still snarled into knots, and tipped the dark jewel into her hand.

She gazed at it, utterly stunned at what she'd done. Humans rarely saw the point of storm-stones. But vampires believed they were sacred.

On impulse, Flora held the jewel to her cheek to feel the familiar tingling disturbance against her skin.

She shut her eyes and saw herself, aged two or three, playing with her mother's jewellery. She heard her own delighted yells as she spotted the storm-stone. 'Mine! Mine!' She smelled her mum's perfume, light and spring-like, faintly mysterious. And for a heartstopping moment she heard her mother's voice. But it came and went like an evening breeze, so faint and fleeting, Flora couldn't catch the words.

She didn't hate Joe's mum or anything. Flora just wished she'd leave her alone. Geraldine was so obviously dying to have thrilling mother–daughter heart-to-hearts, but the thought made Flora feel totally trapped.

She didn't need a new mother. It was her own mum she missed. Now she'd gone, Flora wasn't sure she even belonged in this world any more.

It was painful growing up vampire all by yourself, in a world where humans denied your existence, or worse, saw you as some weirdo who hung around graveyards, thirsting for human blood.

Tat was still too small to confide in. Even Joe didn't really understand who and what Flora truly was. It was as if when her mother died, part of Flora had to die too.

Betty Einstein jumped down from the bed and strolled over to sniff the jewel.

Flora blinked away tears. 'You can see forked lightning, look!' she whispered.

The instant she saw the storm-stone in the museum, Flora felt a sweet rush of home-coming. She hadn't planned to take it, not then. But on the way out, as she passed all those sad forgotten exhibits, she had an overwhelming desire to show it to Clare. It didn't seem wrong at the time. It felt like something she had to do.

But now, alone in her room, she began to feel uneasy.

'It's not hurting anyone,' Flora told the little cat. 'No one's even going to know.'

She'd see how Clare reacted to the jewel first. Then, if it felt right, and if Flora didn't lose her nerve, she might risk some vague comment about her real mum having an unusual background. She'd just take it step by step and see how it went.

Clare was special. Flora had sensed it right away, even before she saw that tell-tale white scar, like a tiny radiant sun, on Clare's golden brown skin. She was smart and funny, and unlike some girls, Clare didn't hide her brains to make the other kids like her. 'They can like me or lump me,' she said cheerfully.

Flora wanted her and Clare to be real friends. Which

meant she'd have to stop pretending to be something she wasn't. You didn't deserve a best friend if you kept lying to them. At least, not a friend like Clare.

Watched by a fascinated Betty Einstein, Flora fastened the stone round her neck, carefully tucking it under her T-shirt. Then she gathered the cat into her arms, hugging her fiercely. 'I'll show Clare tomorrow, then I'll put it back, I swear,' she said into her fur.

But next day Clare's brother came to school alone, his swollen eyes hidden behind dark glasses.

Clare Ying had fallen into a deep and deadly sleep from which no one could wake her. The mysterious sleeping sickness had claimed another victim.

3
The ghoul

Kevin shot awake and groaned. He was late for school again.

He dashed downstairs, pulling on his sweatshirt as he went. To his surprise, his mum was up and dressed to kill in a glittering ball-dress.

'Breakfast's ready,' she beamed.

Kevin gazed around the kitchen in wonder. She must have been cooking all night. There were roast chickens, juicy sides of beef, pink slabs of ham and a pile of sausages, fried golden-brown. Also, Black Forest gateau and a huge lemon meringue pie!

'What's this in aid of?' he breathed.

'Well, it *is* the most important meal of the day,' she said brightly.

Kevin was touched. 'Thanks, Mum. But save it till tonight, yeah? I'm really late.'

He grabbed his coat, wondering why the numbers on the hall clock were the wrong way round.

Outside in the street, everything looked much the same as normal.

That is, until Kevin glanced up and saw the moon; not a flimsy phantom moon, left from the night before, but a buttery yellow globe, floating in a cloudless morning sky.

'Oh, wha-at!' he groaned. 'It's just a stupid dream.'

Kevin's words broke some kind of spell. In eerie slow motion, his dream street began to crumble. Through the wreckage streamed the harsh sunlight of another world. He clambered over the rubble, squinting through the glare.

He seemed to be standing on the edge of a desert. Blinding white sand rippled away into the distance like an inland sea. A punishing wind scoured the dunes, bringing fierce dry heat, choking dust, and the screams of frightened children.

Kevin started to run. Dream or not, those children needed his help.

Suddenly someone came running frantically towards him. Kevin was amazed to recognise Flora's friend, Clare. She seemed terrified.

Then something loomed out of the dust; the hooded figure of something no longer human. In a few effortless strides, Clare's pursuer caught up with her. 'Help!' she screamed, as it began to drag her back towards the desert. 'You've got to help us, Kevin!'

'I'm coming!' he yelled. Then everything went blank, and

Kevin was thrashing around in bed, yelling his head off.

Kevin's nightmare haunted him all the way to school. The danger had felt absolutely real.

It wasn't till break that he noticed several faces were missing from his English group.

Kevin nudged Spoon. 'Where is everyone?'

Spoon's eyes bulged. 'Where've you been hiding, mate? It's been on the news and everything.' He shook his head. 'Makes you wonder who'll be next.'

Kevin stared. 'You mean this sleeping sickness is for real!'

Spoon dropped his voice. 'We're not meant to know this, but I heard they might shut down the school.'

At dinner-time, Kevin dumped his tray on Joe and Flora's table with a crash.

'What happened to football practice?' asked Joe.

'I'm not in the mood, OK,' he growled.

Then he saw that Flora had been crying.

She seemed to make an effort to pull herself together. 'That's a first,' she said, trying to joke. 'What's up?'

Kevin slumped into a seat. 'Don't laugh. I had this stupid dream. I can't get it out of my head.'

Joe and Flora exchanged glances. 'Flora's got this theory,' Joe explained. 'She doesn't think –' He glanced around anxiously. 'She doesn't think the sleeping beauty bug is an illness.'

For the first time Kevin registered that Flora, always pale, was almost grey with shock. He felt a prickle of anxiety. 'What's wrong, Flo?'

'It's Clare,' she whispered. 'They can't wake her up. Her brother said she looks fine. He says it's like she just isn't there. And I think –' Flora gave a shrill little laugh. 'Boy, this is going to sound really crazy. But I think someone is stealing these kids away, in their dreams.'

Kevin's stomach lurched. 'In their dreams,' he echoed. 'Like a kind of evil Pied Piper, you mean?'

Flora gave him one of her probing vampire looks. 'You know something, don't you?' she said accusingly.

'Not really. It's just – Clare was in my dream.'

Flora looked outraged. 'In your dream! But you don't even know her!'

'That's what makes it so weird,' Kevin agreed.

Two third-year girls sat down at their table. 'Don't stop,' sneered one. 'You're having such a deeply riveting conversation.'

Kevin got to his feet, scowling. 'We're all out of rivets,' he said.

'Besides,' Flora said sweetly, 'now you can have your own shallow little conversation, without feeling inferior.'

Flora and Joe followed Kevin outside. And in a quiet corner of the playground, he told them his dream.

'You're absolutely sure it was Clare?' said Flora.

'Positive.'

Joe frowned. 'And that hooded whatever was dragging her into the desert against her will?'

'No question. She was pleading with me to help her.'

'It was a ghoul,' Flora blurted.

'A what?' said Joe.

Flora looked as if she might be sick. 'Mum told me about them. Ghouls are like ghosts. They've been dead so long, they've forgotten they ever had souls. They love to hang around anything evil,' Flora dropped her voice to a whisper, 'which makes them ideal servants for You Know Who.'

Kevin frowned. 'Aren't we getting a bit carried away? I mean stealing kids in their dreams, that's a bit drastic.'

'Vasco stole children's dreams, don't forget,' Joe reminded him.*

'Yeah, because kids' dreams have special magic qualities. He was just like, upgrading his own powers. But why steal actual kids?'

'I don't know,' Flora admitted.

'I suppose, to use them in some way,' suggested Joe.

There was an uneasy silence.

'Supposing you're right,' said Kevin at last. 'I mean, I'm as useful as the next man. How come the ghoul didn't steal me?'

Flora gave him a watery smile. 'I'm working on it. Tell us

*The Dream Snatcher

your dream again, Kev. And don't leave out a thing.'

With some embarrassment, Kevin described his dream: his false awakening, his mum's unusual leisure-wear, the five-star super-de-luxe breakfast, and the hall clock with its backward facing numbers.

Kevin could see Joe was dying to laugh. But Flora took the whole thing incredibly seriously. 'So when did you actually *know* you were dreaming?'

'That's easy!' he said. 'When I saw the moon.'

Flora's eyes gleamed. 'Ha! The moon was your marker.'

'You've lost me,' said Kevin, baffled. 'Must be a —'

'Yes, Kevin, it *is* a vampire thing. Dreaming is a vampire art form, remember? And Mum said, any time I had a nightmare, I should look out for a marker.'

'OK,' said Kevin. 'Now you've just got to tell me what a marker is, and we're home and dry.'

'It can be anything you like, dummy. A word, a shoe, a colour. So long as it's something which reminds you that it's a dream. It looks like you found yours by accident. Just as well,' Flora added darkly.

Kevin felt a twinge of alarm. 'You mean, if I hadn't seen the moon and twigged what was going on, that hooded horror would have dragged me into the desert, along with Clare?'

She nodded. 'To start with, you believed everything you saw, didn't you?'

He shrugged. 'I suppose.'

'Well, maybe Clare's dream didn't seem like a dream to her, either. Maybe to begin with, her pied piper ghoul looked like someone she knew. Then by the time she realised what was happening, it was too late.'

Joe shuddered. 'I'll never sleep again.'

'Why's that then, Joe?' inquired Kevin cheerfully.

'Are you kidding! Someone actually got inside your mind and concocted this spooky dream replica of your life! Not only that, it almost had you fooled.'

'Yeah, but then I saw the moon, didn't I?' said Kevin in the same cheerful tone. 'So if it happens again, I'll just look out for my old whatsit, my marker, and I'll be OK! So will you guys!'

Joe looked anxious. 'But I don't know what my marker is,' he wailed.

'Use mine then, you dummy,' said Kevin.

'Will it work, if I use Kevin's?' Joe asked his sister. 'I mean, can people share the same marker?'

She sighed. 'Use the same one. Use a different one. Who cares, if it does the trick? It's not like the moon's going to wear out, Joe!'

But Joe still seemed uneasy. 'So, if we see the moon or whatever, and realise we're dreaming, does that mean Kevin's desert ghoul has absolutely no power over us?'

Flora frowned. 'I think so. You'd be able to wake up at least.'

'You don't sound very sure,' said Joe anxiously.

'Come on, man, you heard what the king said,' Kevin joked. 'We're the superheroes who save the world. Well, supposing the shiny bright T-shirts win this time around.'

'Oh,' said Joe. 'Maybe that's why Vasco sent –' He stopped in confusion.

'Maybe Vasco sent what?' Flora said at once.

'Er, nothing,' said Joe.

'Liar,' said his sister. 'You're doing that sheep face you always do when you feel guilty.'

Kevin grinned at Joe. 'She's such a sweet girl.'

'I certainly am not,' she snapped.

After school, the friends hurried home, trying not to look at passers-by.

Flora was still deathly pale. 'I had to go to the nurse, to get some aspirin,' she said, 'and I overheard her saying there's six more kids off school with this sleeping bug.'

'Spoon heard ten, not counting Clare,' said Kevin.

A woman came out of the park with a toddler in a buggy. She passed them at a brisk pace, heading towards the traffic lights. Her little girl crooned contentedly to herself. Suddenly she stopped singing, and craned around in her buggy, almost as if she was looking for someone.

Kevin felt Flora stiffen. 'Keep walking,' she hissed.

But at that moment he spotted a tiny teddy bear lying on the ground. He returned it hastily to the little girl, feeling giddy with relief.

'Zombie toddlers would have been too much,' he said shakily.

'I hate this,' Joe muttered. 'Not knowing who's for real.'

'It is a bit stressful,' Kevin agreed. He gave Joe a hard stare. 'Come on. What's this dark secret? I thought we were your mates!'

Joe went red. 'Not out here,' he whispered. 'In the house.'

They went straight up to Joe's room. He fished an envelope out of a drawer. 'This came on the first day of term.'

'*A warning to Joe Quail*,' Kevin read aloud. 'Ooh. Nice.'

'I thought you sent it, remember? You said it was probably Vasco.'

Flora's eyes held a dangerous glint. 'Vasco sent you a warning and you didn't bother telling me!'

'I thought it was a joke,' Joe pleaded. 'And you were all psyched-up about the new school —'

'Stop wittering, Joe, and show us what's inside,' she interrupted.

Joe tipped the envelope upside down. A fine grey powder spilled out.

'This,' he said miserably. 'Next time I went to read it, it just crumbled into dust.'

'What did it say?' said Kevin.

'It said, "darkness will rule". Then the message changed to something like, "light will shine". Vasco must have taken it from that book of prophecy Alice showed us. It's like what you said, Kevin. Maybe the good T-shirts will win, maybe not. There's no way of knowing.'

'I can't *believe* you didn't tell me,' Flora fumed. 'A great brother you are!'

Kevin got the feeling she was really hurt.

'I was going to,' Joe pleaded. 'Then I thought Vasco might have sent it to me for a reason.' He looked away. 'I didn't want to let him down.'

Kevin felt sorry for him. ' 'Course not,' he said. 'I'd have done the same. Vasco probably didn't want to warn us openly. He didn't know who might be watching.'

'But why Joe?' Flora fretted. 'What's so special about him?'

'Vasco was probably in a tearing hurry, disappearing Dream Catchers and going undercover. Maybe my name was just the one he remembered first.'

Flora didn't seem to be listening. 'We should go and see Alice.'

'That's what I don't understand,' said Joe. 'Clare's an Afterdark kid, right?'

Flora glowered. 'What's your point, Joe?'

'Well, when Vasco was in the dream-snatching business, Alice got on his case right away. So why didn't she save Clare?'

'You don't get it, do you?' sighed Kevin. 'Everything's

changed, Joe. Forget those little kiddiwink adventures we used to have. We're all grown-up now.'

Joe stared at them, and the blood drained from his face.

'Kevin's right,' said Flora bleakly. 'This time, it's up to us.'

4
The ruined city

Joe was having one of the worst nights of his life. He'd drift into a state of drowsiness, then shoot awake, heart racing.

He told himself he was imagining things. There was no one watching him. Those shadows were always there. The creaks were just the normal sounds of an old house, settling for the night.

But it seemed that lurking underneath the new improved High School Joe was the same sad headcase who used to believe in the bogey-man.

He thumped his pillow. 'Oh, yes, your majesty!' he said bitterly. 'We would absolutely love to go into mortal danger, your majesty!'

Joe must have been out of his mind! He'd been so impressed to see himself in an ancient prophecy, he had no idea what he was saying.

But he knew now all right. Enough to know he was way, WAY out of his depth.

Flora was right to be mad with him. All that stuff about

not letting Vasco down. Who was he kidding? The truth was, Joe already felt horrendously overstretched; first adjusting to a new family, and now coping with a bewildering new school. Real life was wearing him out, and he simply couldn't cope with another terrifying magical adventure on top.

He sat up in a panic and saw his face in the shadowy mirror.

What's so special about Joe?

He was crazy to think he could be that boy in the book. Not only was Joe far too short to be a hero, but he had no heroic qualities, full stop.

Flora was a ruthless genius. Kevin was quick-witted and brave. Joe was just – weird.

He stared uneasily at his reflection. There was no getting away from it. Those were definitely the eyes of a weird person. He hastily snapped off the light and dived under the covers so he wouldn't have to look at them gleaming in the dark. Finally, worn out with worry, he slipped into a troubled sleep.

As soon as he woke next day, Joe shot across to the window to inspect the sky. To his relief, there was no moon, just autumn sunlight, pouring its tawny honey everywhere. He checked his alarm-clock to be on the safe side, but the numbers seemed fine.

He crept warily on to the landing. No one was yelling

this morning. Nor was there one of those complicated family silences. Just a soft buzz of conversation, Betty Einstein's yowls, and Tat's gruff little voice, singing her yummy yummy breakfast song.

Joe caught snatches of talk as he came downstairs.

'I thought at first I was missing my old study,' Tom was saying anxiously. 'Now I'm worried it's because I'm too happy. What if I'm some kind of sad git writer, who only writes when he's miserable?'

A hint of laughter crept into Joe's mum's voice. 'I suppose I'd have to start being mean to you!' Her tone softened. 'When we get our own place, you'll start writing again. I know you will.'

'And you don't mind about those fancy golden fireplaces?'

Joe's mum giggled. 'I just want you to be happy, Tom Neate, don't you know that yet!'

Joe gave a tactful cough and went in. 'Hi!' he said.

He was on his third piece of toast by the time Flora showed up.

'Deceptively spacious,' Tom mused. 'What does that *mean*? Do they do it with mirrors or something?'

Flora kissed the top of his head. 'It means it's roomier than you think, you nutcase.' She sounded cheerful enough, but Joe saw she had shadows under her eyes.

'Oh, like a Tardis!' Tom said at once. 'Excellent. I could have a different study for every day of the week!'

Using Tom's awful jokes for cover, Joe gave his sister a nudge. 'Hope you did your safety check. No backward numbers, no Black Forest gateaux and definitely no moon.'

Flora glanced furtively at their parents. 'I never got to sleep,' she whispered. 'I kept thinking he was in our house, watching me.' She swallowed a yawn. 'Then I started remembering every horrible thing I've ever done.'

'What kind of things?'

His sister looked evasive. 'Just things. Hurting people's feelings. Stuff like that.' She swallowed. 'I tried thinking about something, you know, positive. But it was the horrible thoughts which seemed true somehow. I kept thinking, "No wonder no one likes you, Flora Neate. You're a spiteful little cow." ' Flora shuddered. 'It was like being haunted.'

Joe could have hugged her. 'Tell me about it!' He was just thinking how blissfully normal things seemed by daylight, when he caught sight of Flora's breakfast. 'Do you *have* to eat beetroot this early?'

'I do, actually. Not sleeping makes me need more vampire vitamins, if you must know.'

'So,' said Joe's mum brightly. 'Have you two got plans today, or do you fancy coming into town with us?'

'Oh, we'd *love* to,' said Flora. She pulled a wistful face. 'But we've got this history project, haven't we, Joe?'

' 'Fraid so,' he agreed hastily. 'Got to go and check out the museum.'

'Oh, we'd *love* to,' Joe mimicked, as they ran down the street. 'What was that about?'

Flora scowled. 'I was trying to be nice to her,' she said.

'That's a first,' he snorted.

Kevin was waiting outside his house. He nodded at the sky. 'So far, so good,' he commented.

'Don't forget you're telling Alice about that warning, Joe,' said Flora in her bossiest tone.

'I suppose,' he said reluctantly.

'You see, deep down in his warped magician's brain, Vasco thinks he's protecting his beautiful princess,' Kevin explained. 'But Alice is like, a really *modern* princess, Joe. She can protect herself. She needs to make up her own mind.'

'I said I'd do it,' growled Joe. 'You don't have to keep on.'

'Oooh,' said Kevin. 'Touchy!'

'Poor little lamb chop. He had a bad night,' Flora jeered, as if Joe wasn't there.

'Like you didn't!' he snapped.

But the minute they entered the museum courtyard, their bad tempers evaporated. The air was so still Joe could hardly breathe. His skin prickled with magic.

'Mum told me about places like this,' Flora said softly. 'Places where the worlds touch.'

'Don't they touch everywhere?' asked Kevin.

'They do,' she agreed. 'But there are these special places called portals. Doorways between worlds.'

'And you reckon this is one of them?' said Kevin.

Flora's eyes glinted. 'I know it is.'

'Think I'd have liked your mum,' Kevin said unexpectedly.

Flora looked touched. 'Yes. You would.'

This morning they had no problems getting inside. Flora simply lifted the latch and the door swung open.

Joe pushed past. 'I'll go first. You two wait here till I say.'

He charged upstairs before he could lose his nerve.

Alice was at her desk, studying the old map he'd noticed before. 'Hi, Joe,' she said, without turning round.

He took a deep breath. 'I've got to tell you something.'

She listened to his confession. Then she sighed. 'Vasco is impossible! You must have been scared to death.'

'Not really,' he lied. 'You're not mad I didn't tell you before?'

'Of course not. You were trying to do the right thing.' Alice gave him a searching look. 'Bad night?'

Joe didn't think he could bear it if Alice ever guessed what a wimp he was. He grabbed a book from her pile, gabbling the first rubbish which came into his head. 'Phew! This is huge. Does everyone do riddles in Afterdark?'

'Oh, that isn't for my exams. Vasco and I were trying to find –' She stopped. 'On second thoughts. I'll wait till the others get here.'

'We're here already,' Kevin called. 'We were just being tactful.'

Flora and Kevin joined them, and Alice fetched them drinks.

Joe took a cautious sip of the ruby-coloured liquid. 'It's sort of Christmassy.' A fizzy warmth began to spread through his body.

'It's an old Afterdark remedy. Especially good after a sleepless night.'

'So how have *you* been sleeping?' Kevin asked.

Alice smiled. 'Not well. This is all much too worrying. But I'm not in any danger. He's only interested in children under fourteen. After that they're no use.'

Joe felt a flicker of fear. 'No use for what?'

Alice spread her map on the floor. 'It's a long story.'

The children crowded round her. Joe caught Alice's familiar scent, summery and mysterious.

'This is where it all began, long, long ago.'

Flora smoothed creases out of the map. 'It looks like some kind of city.'

'It used to be,' said Alice, 'a very wonderful city. There has never been another like it since time began.' Her voice was dreamy.

'What was it called?' asked Kevin.

'No one remembers its true name. When I was small, we just called it the ruined city.'

'So who built it?' asked Joe.

'Children,' Alice said. 'Wise, magical children.'

Kevin looked astonished. 'A bunch of kids built a city by themselves?'

'The children appeared at the very dawn of our world. They lived contentedly for many hundreds of years. Then one day they vanished. No one knows where they went or why. As time passed, people forgot the city ever existed. Eventually it was remembered only as a kind of fairytale.' Alice gave them a shy grin. 'Whenever I got into trouble when I was a little girl, I used to dream of running away to this magical children's city. Vasco says he did too! But like all Afterdark children, we eventually stopped believing in its existence, the way children from this world stop believing in the tooth fairy or Santa Claus.'

'But the city does exist, doesn't it?' said Kevin. 'Or you wouldn't be telling us about it now.'

'Yes. The city does exist.'

Flora's face lit up. 'That's great!' Her smile faded. 'Isn't it?'

Instead of replying, Alice went on with her story.

'The children who built the city were determined to keep it safe from the grown-up world. They suspected that not all adults would respect a city which was run by children.'

'They were right there,' Kevin agreed.

'So they sealed their city with enchantments so strong, that if any adult entered without a child's permission, the entire place would instantly fall into ruins and the intruder would be imprisoned there until the end of time.'

Kevin pulled a face. 'Sounds a bit harsh.'

'Perhaps. But it worked. Everyone knew about the no-adults law. And for hundreds of years, no one tried to break it, ever.' Alice shook back her hair. 'How much Afterdark history do you know?'

'Not much,' said Flora.

'None,' said Joe.

'So you probably didn't know that Afterdark once had two royal families, the Midnights and the Shines. My real Afterdark family name is actually Alice Midnight.'

'It does sound a bit Afterdark-y for this world,' Joe agreed.

Alice grinned. 'Just a bit. Anyway, the Midnights were the word wizards, poets and diplomats. The Shines were our warriors and defenders.' Alice sighed. 'At least, that's how it was meant to be.'

'Don't tell me. The two families had a big bust-up,' said Kevin.

'Worse than that. A few years before I was born, members of both families plotted together to overthrow the kingdom. They succeeded. And those still loyal to Afterdark were forced into exile.'

'But they won in the end?' said Flora anxiously.

Alice nodded. 'After some years the rebels were defeated and they fled into the desert.'

'So where does this city come in?' asked Joe.

Flora shivered. 'I think I know.'

'And me,' said Kevin grimly. 'After they'd lost the war, those rebels checked out the desert, spied this deserted city that wasn't meant to exist, and decided it was the perfect place for a rebel base.'

Alice looked impressed. 'That's right.'

'How did you know?' asked Joe.

Kevin tapped his skull. 'Science, mate. But the rebels didn't believe in the magic, did they? Plus they hadn't been invited, so – BOSH!'

'Bosh?' echoed Flora faintly.

'There was an earthquake so violent that tremors were felt in every part of Afterdark. It was followed by the worst sandstorm my world has ever seen. By the time it died down, the city had become a desolate ruin –'

'And the rebels were trapped for ever,' Joe whispered.

'No one in Afterdark was too worried at first,' said Alice. 'It suited them perfectly to have their enemies conveniently trapped in a prison of their own making. In fact, they started sending criminals and troublemakers there on a regular basis.'

Kevin winced. 'Oops.'

'Quite,' said Alice. 'One of them was a very dangerous and devious sorcerer.'

Kevin sat up. 'You're talking about our one, aren't you? The evil pied piper who's kidnapping kids and spying on us through old ladies, and — and pigeons.'

Alice nodded unhappily.

'What's he like?' Flora's voice was suddenly sharp with tension.

'In many ways he is like a child himself. A heartless precocious child. He —'

'I mean what does he look like?' Flora interrupted. 'Old, young, fat, thin? Black, white, green?'

'Why do you care?' Joe asked irritably.

Flora had gone white. 'I want to know what kind of monster stole my friend Clare!'

Alice sighed. 'I wish I could tell you. The truth is, he uses so many disguises, I doubt if the magician himself remembers his true face.'

Flora shivered. 'Don't. That's too creepy.'

'You did ask,' Kevin pointed out.

'He has to have a name at least,' said Joe.

'He has several extremely impressive names,' agreed Alice. 'All entirely of his own invention. But his true name was also lost long ago.'

Kevin looked uneasy. 'So what did the magician with no name get up to in the lost city?'

'By day he searched among the ruins,' said Alice. 'At night he'd pore over his findings in the firelight; scraps of ancient riddles, fragments of painted marble, remnants of faded cloth.'

Joe's scalp crept. 'What was he looking *for*?'

'A key,' she said. 'A magical code, something, anything which would unlock the secrets of the ruined city, but with him as its master.'

'Did he want to rebuild it or something?' Joe asked.

'Yes,' said Alice. 'But with one difference. The original city was a kind of paradise. His would be a place of never-ending nightmares.'

'It doesn't sound incredibly groovy now,' Kevin pointed out.

'It has no real power to do harm. Not yet.'

Joe stared uneasily at the map. Then he heard what Alice said. 'What do you mean, not yet?' he demanded.

'The magician has one problem. The clues scattered around the city were devised by children. And though he is *like* a child in many ways, he can't actually understand how children, even magical children, think. So he made up his mind to get some help.'

They stared at her, electrified.

In the sudden hush, Joe heard the river lazily lapping against its banks below.

Alice stood up. 'Now do you see?'

Joe's mouth was dry. 'He's stealing children from our world and forcing them to try to crack the code.'

Kevin looked disgusted. 'No wonder they were crying and screaming.'

'But it breaks just about every cosmic law!' cried Flora. 'How is it even possible?'

'The first time, it was probably an accident. With his body imprisoned in the desert, the magician grew incredibly bored. At last, all that restless intelligence broke free. Short trips at first, to spy on his enemies. But he grew steadily more skilful, until soon he was able to mind-travel wherever he chose.'

'The zombie-grams,' breathed Kevin.

Alice looked grave. 'Then as time went on, he acquired new and more deadly skills.'

'He got into children's dreams,' Flora whispered.

They had never seen Alice so troubled. 'Can you imagine what such a being will be capable of, if he discovers the key?' she asked them.

Kevin sucked in his breath. 'That guy's got to be stopped. No question.'

Flora's eyes blazed. 'We've got to figure out that code before he does. We've got to go NOW!' She sounded almost hysterical.

'What, actually go to – to the ruined city?' Joe stuttered.

'It's our only hope, Joe,' his sister said. 'We've got to steal its secrets from right under that magician's nose.'

And with a jolt of terror, Joe understood why this quest

would be different from all the others. He felt it in his clammy hands and racing heartbeat. He saw it in Flora's eyes.

It was because this time, they might never come back.

5
The gate of nightmares

They hastily got ready for their mission to the ruined city.

Alice checked her list of supplies. 'Water bottles, map, torch, knife.'

Joe struggled into his clothes. They were unlike anything he'd worn in Alice's world before; dark, baggy and softly padded, with ties at wrists and ankles. There was also a strange cap which pulled right over his face, so that only his eyes showed. Joe inspected himself in the mirror.

'Eek! I look scary.' He took it off again.

Alice grinned. 'Afterdark fighting clothes. Great to move in. Also useful for keeping snakes and spiders out.'

Flora became unusually still. 'So, are there like loads of snakes and spiders where we're going?' she inquired casually.

Kevin glanced up from lacing his boots. 'They won't bother us, Flo. We'll be with Alice. She's the Lady of the Beasts, aren't you?'

'Normally,' she agreed. 'Better safe than sorry, though.' She hunted around, found a tiny bottle filled with brownish fluid and popped it into her rucksack. 'Snakebite serum.'

'What do you mean, *normally?*' Kevin demanded. 'Why would desert creepy crawlies be different to any other kind?'

'The magician might have nobbled them,' Flora explained. 'Turned them into his creepy slaves, sort of thing. They're called "familiars", if you're interested.'

'Nice,' said Kevin. 'Any more surprises we should know about?'

Alice patted his stubbly head. 'Probably.'

He groaned. 'I *knew* she was going to say that!'

It was weird. They were about to go into the lair of a cruel and heartless magician, yet everyone was kidding about as if they couldn't wait to get cracking.

Alice stuffed her cap into her pocket. 'I hate these things. I never put mine on till the last minute.' Somehow in her baggy fighting clothes, the Afterdark princess managed to look even lovelier than ever.

A pang shot through Joe's heart and he knew he'd die for her if necessary.

'Ready?' Alice asked calmly.

'As we'll ever be,' said Kevin.

At Alice's touch the mirror grew bright and fluid, and once again the children crossed into the world of Afterdark.

They were inside some kind of military camp. Warriors of both sexes practised ferocious moves, or buffed up weapons and groomed the horses. Among them, Joe recognised trolls, giants and dryads, as well as other strange beings completely unknown to him. It seemed that all Afterdark's magical races had sent troops to defend their world. But the majority of the warriors were vampires.

Joe had known for ages that Afterdark vampires were nothing like the late night horror film variety, but it was rather overwhelming, seeing so many together. They were all just that bit too perfect-looking. And they had so much energy; laughing and gesturing and talking at once. Not for the first time, Joe felt grateful his sister was only half-vampire.

The warriors spotted Alice immediately. The children followed her shyly, with warriors bowing low on either side, so that Joe felt as if he was walking through a wheatfield in a high wind.

They were making their way towards a long, high wall. Elaborate gates were set into it, with the moonlit beauty which Joe associated with Afterdark. But these struck him as slightly sinister.

'They're not made from nightingales, are they?' he asked uneasily.

Flora pulled her don't ask face.

'That's never ivory?' said Kevin.

Alice sighed. 'Afterdark poets say our false dreams enter through the gates of ivory. True dreams come through the gates of horn.'

'So we're going through the lying and cheating gate?' said Kevin.

She nodded. 'Also the gate of nightmares and illusions.'

Flora gave a squeak of excitement. 'I don't believe it!' She raced into the crowd and Joe saw her throw her arms around a huge pirate with dreadlocks so thick and knotted that they looked like tree roots.

Kevin broke into a big grin. 'Never thought I'd see Spinner again.'

'Me neither,' said Joe.

Suddenly the dream ranger was crushing Joe in an enormous bear hug, and Joe found himself breathing in the heartbreakingly sweet scent of the dream fields.

Flora wouldn't let go of Spinner's arm. 'What are you *doing* here?'

Spinner's eyes glittered. 'The same as you, little daughter. When I heard what was happening, I came straight away.'

'Because of the magician, you mean?' said Joe.

'I've seen some wickedness in my line of work, but using children as slaves —' Unusually, Spinner seemed lost for words.

Joe thought he knew another reason for the ranger's distress. Last time they met, he had been searching for his five daughters who had disappeared in mysterious circumstances.

'Didn't you ever find your —?' Joe began. But something in Spinner's eyes stopped him finishing his sentence.

The ranger stared fiercely into the distance. 'I haven't given up hope,' he said quietly. 'I never give up hope.'

Joe noticed Alice chatting to a group of alarmingly under-dressed trolls. She waved. 'There are some people I want you to meet,' she called.

'We'd better go,' said Flora reluctantly.

'Yeah, later, Spinner,' said Kevin. They ran off into the crowd.

Spinner caught at Joe's sleeve. 'I want to talk to you.'

'I'll be over in a minute!' Joe yelled to the others. 'What's up?'

'We'll walk a bit,' said Spinner. 'You never know who's listening.'

The ranger slung his arm around Joe's shoulders as they walked. 'How much do you know about this magician?'

'Not much. Sounds scary though,' Joe admitted. Then he turned red. Now Spinner would think he was a wimp.

But the ranger's next words took Joe by surprise. 'You're right to be scared. Being brave has nothing to do with not being scared.'

Joe gulped. 'Doesn't it?'

'Nothing,' said Spinner. 'Just so long as when it comes to the crunch, you remember to be your big self, and not your small self.'

'My what self?' asked Joe.

'The big self sees the big picture,' Spinner explained. 'It

sees patterns in stars. But the small self can only focus on one feeble star at a time.'

Joe would bet serious money that Spinner had never been a one-star-at-a-time person. Everything about him was larger than life. His laugh, his temper, his elaborate dreadlocks; they all crackled with energy, so that just by standing next to him Joe felt new courage flowing into his veins.

'Spinner,' he said anxiously. 'Did you ever feel like you'd really cracked something? Only it turned out you were just going round in circles, having to do the same scary stuff again and again?'

Spinner nodded gravely. 'Yes.'

'That's it,' Joe said hastily. 'That's all I wanted to know.'

Spinner frowned. 'It's not circles, Joe. More like spirals. It isn't *exactly* the same stuff, you see. You're learning each time. And each time it comes round again, you learn that bit faster.'

He gave a roar of laughter. 'Must be getting old! Giving youngsters advice. Here, this is far more useful.' Spinner reached into his ancient jacket and slipped something into Joe's hand. 'There's times when a humble slingshot can make all the difference.'

Joe was touched. 'Thanks, Spinner.'

Spinner frowned. 'One more thing. I'd steer clear of the bird-people, Joe, if I was you.'

Joe felt a prickle of dismay.

'They don't strictly live inside the city,' Spinner explained. They live up in the hills, so I've heard. Terrifying blood-thirsty creatures. People say their children have to fend for themselves as soon as they can walk.' He lowered his voice. 'Some even say they're cannibals.'

Joe swallowed. This mission got more alarming every minute.

Kevin came dashing up. 'Sorry to interrupt, but they're opening the gates.'

Spinner and Joe hurried after him.

As they got closer, Joe saw that the gates were guarded by dozens of belligerent trolls, including the ones he'd seen talking to Alice.

Flora joined them.

'What are those trolls *wearing*?' Joe chortled. 'Apart from war-paint?'

'Not nearly enough, if you ask me,' said Kevin. 'Flora doesn't know where to look, do you, Flo!'

Joe grinned. 'If they go to war dressed like that, I'm surprised they ever need to fight.'

'Hush,' said Spinner sternly. 'Our troll brothers might hear you. For the time being, we must all unite against our common enemy.'

Joe felt himself turn red. 'I didn't mean –'

Flora giggled. 'He's kidding, Joe.'

And Joe saw that Spinner's eyes were glinting with mischief. 'But why do they need to guard the gate? I thought the magician couldn't get out of the city.'

'He can't,' said Flora. 'But he's got all these icky spies and familiars in Afterdark, and they're going frantic trying to join him.' She pulled a face. 'Makes you realise what we're up against.'

'How come you're so cool, Kev?' Joe teased.

Kevin shrugged. 'You forget, I've actually seen this city. I just want to put a stop to all this. Put a stop to it for good and all.'

'These gates must be incredibly heavy,' Alice was saying admiringly.

'Incredibly heavy, your highness,' agreed the largest troll. 'It's extremely taxing work, is this gate-minding business.'

'You got to have the right physique,' one of his companions chipped in.

'Got to eat the right food,' said a third troll, puffing out his chest. 'I'd go so far as to say, you got to think the right thoughts, even.'

Flora was trying to keep a straight face. 'The trolls were being really huffy,' she explained. 'They were convinced everyone was looking down on them. But Alice totally won them round.'

'I can see,' said Joe.

The princess began shaking hands warmly with each

troll in turn. By the time she'd finished, they were all blushing like poppies.

'Such a lovely girl,' one troll murmured to his friend. 'Her voice is sweeter than my mammy's, and she was famed for her speaking voice, my mammy was.'

'How *sweet!*' Flora breathed. 'I'll never be mean about trolls again.'

'What does he mean, his mammy's voice?' Joe spluttered. 'Every troll I've ever met sounds like he has a bad cold.'

Kevin grinned. 'Do you wonder? Flashing their wobbly bits like that!'

With a mighty straining of muscles, the trolls began to pull back the gates. Suddenly a wild-looking figure darted from the crowd and made a dash for the opening. Five trolls promptly wrestled him to the ground.

Kevin winced. 'What a way to go.'

'The poor creature is beyond caring,' said Spinner.

Joe suspected Spinner was right. He had seen the expression in the familiar's eyes. Nothing human remained, only a burning hunger.

To Joe's dismay, the ranger began to walk away. 'Spinner!' he called. 'Where are you going?'

'Can't stand goodbyes,' yelled the ranger. 'Remember what I said!'

'I'll try,' Joe whispered.

There was no time to feel sad. The gates stood open at

last. There, on the other side, was the desert of Kevin's dream.

'Let's go,' said Alice.

The children followed Alice into the badlands which separated the magician's city from the rest of Afterdark. Joe was the last through the gates. He heard them shut behind him with a horribly final CLANG, but he refused to let himself look round.

They trudged across the sand dunes, stopping only for gulps from their water bottles.

'This stupid wind can't make up its mind,' Kevin grumbled.

Alice looked thoughtful. 'I could fix it. But then he'd know we're here.' She gave a little shrug. 'It's possible he knows we're here anyway. But if he sees unscheduled bursts of magic out here in the badlands, he'll *definitely* know we're here.'

'Then please don't,' Flora pleaded. She made frantic spitting sounds. 'Ugh! I hate getting sand in my teeth.'

Suddenly Joe heard a spine-chilling cry. He ducked in alarm as a big bald bird went flapping over his head.

He had always supposed that deserts were empty places. But as they tramped along, they saw various weird life forms, all apparently thriving in the harsh, dry landscape.

Once Flora fled shrieking from a bizarre horned beetle. 'Is there a rule which says everything in the desert has to look like an alien from outer space?' she shuddered.

Even the weather was weird.

'What *are* those things?' Joe asked, as yet another cloud of dust went whirling past.

'Dust-devils,' said Alice. 'Baby cyclones,' she explained. 'They're quite harmless. Well, usually.'

Joe noticed that Flora was glowering at him. He must have interrupted her private chat with Alice. He pulled a face at Kevin and they hurried out of earshot.

'You couldn't possibly know Clare was going to be abducted,' Alice was saying.

'I'm meant to be her friend,' said Flora huskily. 'She should have been in *my* dream. Not Kevin's. Maybe I could have saved her.' She unstoppered her water bottle and gulped some water. The ache in her throat made it hard to swallow.

'Alice, I've been wanting to ask you something,' she blurted out. 'But you've got to tell me the truth. No matter how horrible it is.'

Flora shut her eyes, and before she could lose her nerve, she gabbled, 'Was it because of knowing me that Clare got caught?'

Alice took a breath.

'I haven't finished,' said Flora. 'Doesn't it strike you as weird? For the first time since I was in infant school, I meet a girl who actually wants to be my friend. And just a few hours later she's in some spooky enchanted sleep.'

'But that wasn't anything to do with you!'

Flora was suddenly blinded with tears. 'It feels like I'm not meant to belong anywhere. It feels like I'm this bad vampire girl who hurts everyone she cares about, just by *knowing* them.'

'I know it does.'

'What if it keeps happening? I'll have to be alone, my whole life! What am I going to *do*, Alice?'

Alice caught at her hand. 'You're doing it. You're setting out on an incredibly dangerous mission to save Clare and the others.'

Flora was almost beside herself. 'You don't get it. Supposing we rescue them? And I really hope we do, Alice,' she choked. 'But I'll still be me. I'll still be the weird girl with this – this dark secret.'

To Flora's amazement, Alice smiled.

Flora glared through her tears. 'What's so funny?'

Alice didn't seem in the least repentant. 'You don't know who you'll be when this mission's over,' she said sensibly. 'Magic changes everything. You of all people should know that. Also, maybe your secret isn't so dark as you think.'

Her eyes glinted. 'I mean, purely as an experiment you could try thinking of it as a *light* secret!'

It's all right for you, Flora was going to say. But at that

moment she spotted something which temporarily made her forget her troubles.

She pulled urgently at Alice's arm. 'Alice, look!'

The sun had grown so fierce that the desert began to swim in front of Joe's eyes. Suddenly, out of this swimmy haze, an oasis appeared.

It was the kind you might see in a picture book, consisting of a few palm trees, some languid camels, and an Arabian Nights-type tent: and Joe knew the moment he saw it that it was too good to be true.

Kevin's eyes lit up. 'I've always wanted to see a mirage!'

This extraordinary illusion was perfect in every detail. The colours were so bright, Joe could almost taste them.

As they got closer, he was puzzled to hear splashing sounds coming from the tent. 'Mirages don't have soundtracks, do they?' he hissed.

'Anything's possible in Afterdark,' grinned Kevin.

Very stealthily, he lifted the tent flap and they peeped in.

Inside, the fragrance of scented oils drifted through the air. Someone had draped lustrous silks across a screen, creating a rosy glow. Half-hidden behind the screen was an old-fashioned bathtub. Bubbles spilled frothily over the sides, the way they do in old films.

Joe felt a rush of horrible embarrassment. Dangling gracefully over the edge of the bath was a slender foot with brightly-painted toenails. Whoever was in the bath began humming dreamily.

Kevin let go of the tent flap as if it had bitten him. 'Flaming Norah,' he muttered.

The humming stopped. 'Bye, boys,' teased the bubble bath girl in a breathy voice. 'Do drop by again!'

And like an outsize soap bubble, the mirage disappeared.

Joe and Kevin exchanged uneasy glances.

'We've been made to look totally stupid,' said Kevin. 'I'm not impressed.'

They glanced nervously down the trail. Alice and Flora were still deep in conversation. 'I don't think they noticed,' whispered Joe.

'Then don't mention it,' suggested Kevin. 'They'll think we're, you know, at that age.'

Joe grinned. 'Kevin, you've always been that age.'

They waited for the girls to catch up.

'You need to splash on some suncream, Kev,' said Flora in her bossiest voice. 'You've gone bright red. Haven't you seen it yet?' she added casually.

To their relief she was pointing far off into the distance.

Joe stared into the glare and finally made out a shadowy outline, rising from the sands. His heart sank. Even from a distance, the city seemed enormous. Where would they start looking for clues in a place so huge?

Then the wind changed direction and cries of distress

drifted through the air, and Joe realised that his worries came from the part of him which could only see one small star at a time. Look at the big picture, Spinner had said. We've come to save the children, he told himself. And that's what we're going to do.

Alice pulled on her cap, so that only her eyes were showing. The children hastily put theirs on too.

'Yikes!' yelled Flora suddenly. 'Everybody down!'

Everyone threw themselves flat.

An enormous dust-devil was heading straight for them, spraying out sand like a gritter lorry. It got to within about a hundred metres, then to their relief, it veered, and whirled harmlessly away.

Joe felt a jolt of fear as he saw what the dust-devil had left behind. A hooded figure, dodging in and out of the dunes.

'It's one of them,' Kevin hissed. 'The ghouls who snatched Clare.'

Joe felt his heart thumping against the sand, as the ghoul padded closer. He'd known they might never get back home. He just hadn't expected things to go wrong so soon. They hadn't even reached the city yet.

A sinister shadow fell across their hiding-place.

Alice didn't seem to move, but suddenly a knife blade flashed in her hand. The ghoul saw the flash and shouted a warning.

'I know that voice,' said Kevin suspiciously.

'So do I,' said Flora.

But Alice just gasped.

The desert ghoul pushed back his hood. And there, laughing back at them, was the impossibly good-looking face of Vasco Shine.

6

Kevin and the multiple choice test

Joe was in an underground cavern, somewhere under the desert.

It was suffocatingly hot. On one side of him was solid rock. On the other was a drop, so sheer that even thinking of it made him dizzy.

Joe could just make out Kevin's stocky shape ahead of him. Without Alice's torch, the darkness would have been total.

Alice and Vasco were in front, having a heated argument.

'Creeping around in that stupid get-up,' Alice was saying. 'What if I'd stabbed you!'

Vasco sounded hurt. 'You don't think I *like* wearing this thing? It simply allows me to blend in.'

'But with *ghouls*, Vasco,' Alice protested.

'Slow down, Flo,' said Kevin. 'We can't all see in the dark, mate.'

Flora waited for them to catch up. 'Sorry. I forgot.'

Vasco's voice floated back through the darkness. 'I

thought you'd be pleased that all my undercover work paid off. Not to mention, if I hadn't found you, you'd still be slogging through the desert.'

'I keep *telling* you, Vee, we weren't lost! I had a map!'

Joe tried not to laugh. 'She's really giving him a hard time.'

'Serves him right for skulking about.' Kevin dropped his voice. 'That's the trouble with Vee. He might have given up being a villain, but he's not a team player, know what I mean?'

'Oh, well, that's vampires for you,' said Flora icily.

'It's got nothing to do with his *species*, Flo. It's what he's like. He's got that — that playboy streak.'

It was true, Joe thought. Vasco had a way of turning life into some dazzling private game.

'Don't you want to know where this tunnel goes?' Vasco wheedled.

Joe grinned. Vasco was going to impress Alice if it killed him!

'OK, Vasco,' she sighed. 'Where does this tunnel go?'

Vasco cheered up. 'You see, this isn't any old cavern. It's actually a kind of ancient subway taking us right into the ruined city. And believe it or not, it finishes up exactly where we need to go.'

'How can you possibly know! We haven't the first idea where those clues are.'

'Ah, but we do, your highness! Because my brilliant short-cut is taking us straight to an extremely fascinating building.'

'What, one that isn't ruined, you mean? Because that's not possible. Absolutely no buildings survived intact.'

'This one did,' said Vasco smugly. 'Which suggests it just *might* be a useful source of magical clues. Our magician certainly thinks so. You wouldn't believe all the activity that's going on up there.'

'Did you hear that, Kev?' breathed Joe.

'He's good,' Kevin agreed reluctantly. 'I'll give him that.'

They were approaching what appeared to be a dead end, but turned out to be a flight of primitive steps carved into the rock.

Alice decided they should rest for a few minutes, before beginning their ascent. 'And Vasco can tell us what he's found out.'

'We heard about that building,' said Flora.

'Excellent news,' said Kevin.

Vasco took a long swig from his water bottle. 'OK. As you know, I've been hanging around the city, seeing what I can find out.'

'Charming information out of the ghouls,' Alice suggested.

'Charming everyone I meet, naturally,' he said airily. 'I've also been doing some exploring, which is how I found out about this building directly overhead. Apparently the children who built it designed it like a huge magical puzzle.'

'Cool,' said Flora.

'More like impossible,' sighed Vasco. 'They covered the walls with magic symbols. Some are false and some are true. Before anyone can access the city's power, they must pick the right ones. Three are needed altogether.'

'It's always three, isn't it?' said Kevin plaintively. 'Three little pigs. Three magic symbols. It's OK, Flo,' he added hastily as Flora took a breath. 'Don't tell me why!'

'I don't know why, *actually*, Kevin,' she snapped. 'I was just going to say it was three children too. You know, in that prophecy.'

Joe patted her shoulder. 'We're the perfect team, that's why.'

'You think?' she said in a sour voice.

'Yes,' he said, surprised. 'Don't you?'

'Oh, don't ask me. Everyone knows vampires are just hopeless at teams.'

'Will you just drop it,' Kevin hissed. 'Vasco's talking.'

'These steps should bring us directly to a secret entrance into the chamber,' Vasco was saying. 'There's one small complication once you get inside the chamber. Most of the symbols are harmless. Others are — not.'

'You mean they could do us some damage?' said Kevin.

'I mean they could kill you,' Vasco said.

Joe's heart gave a thump of fear.

'It's just a rumour,' Vasco said hastily. 'But it's as well to know.'

Kevin frowned. 'But you and Alice will be helping us, right?'

Vasco shook his head. 'Sorry, mate. This chamber was never meant for adult eyes.'

'You must act quickly,' said Alice. 'Vasco says a new child is sent there every half-hour to choose another symbol.'

'That's crazy,' Joe blurted out. 'This magician is some kind of genius. If he hasn't found the right symbols, how can we?'

'You're children,' Vasco reminded him.

'So are all his little slaves!' said Joe bitterly.

'Exactly,' said Alice. 'They're slaves, Joe. You *chose* to come here. Those children didn't. That makes your chances much higher.'

'Oh, let's just get on with it,' Kevin growled.

The long climb through the stifling darkness seemed endless.

The steps weren't really steps, just crude footholds in the cliff-face. One false move and they could be dashed to pieces on the rocks below. Once when Joe lost his footing, Vasco instantly steadied him. Weak with fear, Joe continued to haul himself from step to step.

When they finally reached the top, they waited while Vasco prodded the smooth rock without success. Suddenly he gave a crow of triumph.

With an unpleasant grating sound, a portion of rock slid aside, releasing clouds of ancient dust and an overpowering odour of magic.

Vasco checked his watch. 'You've got twenty minutes before they send in the next child. Good luck!'

'We'll see you back here with the symbols,' said Alice.

Vasco and Alice radiated confidence, but Joe knew they were worried sick underneath.

Big picture, he told himself fiercely. Patterns in the stars. Taking a deep breath, he dived through the door in the rock.

To his surprise, there was light ahead; not sunlight, but a lovely golden haze.

Kevin and Flora appeared beside him.

'At least it's not dark,' whispered Kevin.

'Oh, absolutely,' muttered Flora. 'And being in a deadly chamber of magic tricks and traps is so much nicer.'

'You thought it was cool, earlier,' Kevin pointed out.

But Joe couldn't speak. The chamber was beautiful. It glowed with gold leaf and berry red and that intense blue he'd seen in pictures of Egyptian tombs. What he loved most was how you could actually tell this enchanted place had been created by children.

He could almost feel their magical minds touching his across the centuries. *Come and find us, Joe!*

But it wasn't awe which silenced Joe. It was dismay.

The chamber was vast! And every inch of space throbbed with shapes and patterns of an unmistakably magical kind. There were thousands and thousands of them.

'They've got to be joking,' Flora said at last. 'It's like the fairytale where the girl has to sort out the peas from the whatever. We can't check every one of these in twenty minutes. We can't *reach* most of them!'

'Exactly,' agreed Kevin cheerfully. 'So don't even try.' To Joe's astonishment, he doubled up laughing.

'Kevin?' said Joe. 'Are you OK?'

Kevin grinned. 'I'm not cracking up, if that's what you mean. It just came to me. This is like those multiple choice questions at school.'

'And that made you *laugh*?' said Flora.

'It did, actually. I've got this infallible technique, you see. I just close my eyes, and let Mr Pointy do the work.' Kevin wiggled his finger under Flora's nose.

'You're insane, Kitchener,' said Joe. 'You heard what Vasco said. Some of these symbols could kill us!'

Flora coughed. 'Actually, it's not as stupid as it sounds.' She saw Joe's horrified face. 'No, really. There's this thing in maths, called probability. You use it to calculate risks and stuff. I'd say the odds of coming up with the goods this way are about even.'

'Isn't that a nerdy way of saying we're doomed?' said Joe huskily.

Flora shrugged. 'Do you have a better idea?'

'No.'

Kevin rubbed his hands. 'Enough chat. Let's have some action.'

Joe watched in despair as Kevin and Flora psyched themselves up to choose their symbols. How did they manage to act so normal?

'Get a move on, Quail!' Kevin called.

Get a move on! Joe was so panic-stricken that the walls were blurring in front of his eyes. He couldn't even think straight. How was he meant to choose one meaningless pattern over another?

What if Kevin and Flora got it right and he failed? What if everything Joe loved was destroyed because, he, Joe Quail, made the wrong decision? What if? *What if?* The list of terrible consequences was endless.

Then a strange calm descended on him. What have I got to lose, he thought? If I'm going to die, I might as well die doing the best I can.

Joe shut his eyes and let his finger do the work.

'Wow!' he breathed.

It felt exactly as though someone had attached a piece of invisible thread to his finger. For a thread which wasn't actually there, it had an alarming life of its own. It began tugging him persistently across the chamber.

Eyes still tightly closed, Joe allowed himself to be coaxed

along on the end of that vibrating thread of magic. With the tiniest scrape of his fingernail, his finger collided with a cold, smooth surface.

He cringed, anticipating a sudden and horrible death.

Nothing happened.

Oh-oh, he thought wildly. Maybe you open your eyes, see the symbol and *then* die horribly!

He couldn't bear to look. Then he realised he couldn't bear not to look either. He opened his eyes.

His finger had landed smack-bang on the symbol of a magic eye; an eye with wings. It was painted blue and gold and Joe found it utterly beautiful. It was exactly what he'd have chosen for himself, supposing he'd known it was there.

He stared at it, willing himself to remember each tiny detail. 'Blue, gold, eye, wings,' he muttered. 'Dot squiggle arrow.'

'Joe!' Flora called urgently.

'Just a minute.'

Vasco peered around the secret door. 'Time's up.'

Joe could have laughed. In the end, it had been so easy.

'We did it!' he called in a stage whisper.

'That's great,' said Vasco. 'Now just get back here, OK?'

They began to hurry back towards Vasco and safety, their feet scuffling on the dusty tiles.

They were almost halfway when they heard the cry.

It wasn't a cry of pain or fear, but the sobbing of a small child who has given up hope of ever being comforted.

It was the loneliest sound Joe had ever heard.

The children faltered.

'Hurry up,' Vasco hissed. 'You're cutting this really fine.'

They looked at each other, and without a word, turned back and ran towards the sound.

'Are you crazy!' Vasco pleaded.

'Won't be long, Vee,' Kevin called. 'Got a bit of business to see to.'

The main door stood half-open. The children slipped though the gap.

'Uh-oh,' said Kevin.

Two figures were coming towards them. One was a weeping child in dusty rags. Beside him stalked the hooded shape of a ghoul. 'But I don't know what I'm looking for,' the child whimpered.

They cowered in the shadows, until the ghoul and its distraught prisoner had gone past.

Flora closed her eyes. 'Can we stay here a minute? I feel a bit funny.'

Joe sympathised. Now they had left the magical chamber, he too was feeling the full force of the magician's presence. Like some deadly gas, it came seeping from every part of the ruined city.

Kevin put his arm round Flora. 'Deep breaths,' he said. 'There you go.'

She shuddered. 'It's so creepy how he's like everywhere and nowhere.'

'Don't think about it,' said Kevin. 'Think about saving that little kid. That's what you've got to do.'

But other heart-rending cries drifted into their hiding-place. And now Joe heard a new sound, a feverish rattling and chinking of metal.

Flora pulled herself together. 'This way,' she called.

They raced to the end of the passage. As they stepped out of the shadows, the blast of heat made Joe catch his breath. It was like walking into some huge diabolical oven.

He stood blinking, half-blinded by the glare. They had emerged on a barren hillside, high above the ruined city. Behind them rose the slanting wall of a gigantic pyramid. In front of them was a sight Joe knew he'd remember for the rest of his life.

Under the empty gaze of the magician's ghouls, an army of children worked frantically in the midday heat.

The littlest children sifted through fragments of stone or tile. Older children struggled to lift a shattered statue into an upright position. As they worked, Joe heard over and over again that feverish slither of metal: the rattling of their chains.

Here was the ruined city at last. And these were its slaves.

7

Never-ending noon

The child slaves had a ghostly flickery quality, like TV pictures which needed adjusting. 'It's like they're only half here,' said Joe in dismay.

Kevin sounded disgusted. 'What did you expect! Their other halves are at home, fast asleep. This is like the *dreaming* part. Their souls or whatever.'

'Where are they all from?' Flora whispered.

'Anywhere,' said Kevin bitterly. 'Everywhere.'

Joe felt a thrill of horror. He could hear subdued voices speaking in different languages. The magician was stealing children from all over Joe's world!

And Joe realised they had made a terrible mistake. How could they save all these children? They didn't even know the way home! In their mercy dash to save one child, they had put their entire mission at risk.

Kevin was the first to pull himself together. 'Erm. Don't know if you've noticed, but we're the only kids without our own personal hardware. If one of those ghouls looks up now, we'll stick out like a sore whatsisname.'

Flora looked dazed. 'We've been idiots.'

'It's too late to worry about that,' said Joe to his own surprise. 'The important thing is, what are we going to do now?'

'Yeah,' said Kevin. 'Switch on that vampire vision, Flo.'

Flora gave a brave little nod.

She shaded her eyes, scanning the jumble of ruins. Beyond the crumbling sun-bleached rubble of the city, the desert simmered in its midday haze. In the distance, a lone dust-devil performed its dizzy spiral dance.

'I could be wrong,' she said cautiously, 'but I think I can see an entrance to another tunnel. Right now, no one seems to be watching it.'

'What do you reckon?' Kevin asked.

'I say go for it,' said Joe. Flora nodded.

'One – two – THREE!' commanded Kevin.

They flew down the steps. The sun gave Joe a brief, stinging slap in the face, then he was back in the shadows, his eyes so dazzled that it was a few seconds before he saw they were not alone.

The airless space was crowded with slaves, all tapping and prodding the tunnel walls with a kind of hopeless thoroughness.

The slave children shrank back at their approach.

'They're terrified,' murmured Kevin.

'They probably think they're dreaming us,' said Joe.

'Don't,' shuddered Flora. She held out her hand. 'Don't be scared,' she coaxed. 'We won't hurt you.'

But the slaves just huddled together, as if dreading what these strange apparitions might do to them.

Flora looked as if she might cry. 'But we've come to help you!'

'No one can help us now,' said a child in a dreary voice. 'We've got to be his slaves for ever and ever.'

'You're wrong,' said Joe. 'We're working on getting you all out of here.'

The children shook their heads.

'Uh-uh,' said a little girl sorrowfully. 'Because you're not real. And we're not real either. Nothing's real any more. Didn't you know that?'

Joe felt himself turn cold with fear.

'We should go,' said Kevin urgently. 'We'll end up like them, if we're not careful.'

Flora scowled. 'No. We're here for a reason. I *know* we are.'

Then a voice called, 'Flora! Is that you?'

Flora peered through the gloom in amazement. 'Clare?'

The girls rushed towards each other. At the last minute Clare looked upset. 'Actually I'm not ideal hugging material, just now.'

'Oh, who cares!' shrieked Flora. And carefully embracing

the space around Clare, she gave her two smacking air-kisses. 'Mwah! Mwah!'

Clare didn't know whether to laugh or cry. 'You nutcase,' she said. 'You total and utter nutcase!'

'I was so worried about you. But you look great! Doesn't she look great, Joe?'

Joe nodded, grinning. Clare's dark hair was floury with dust and her clothes were in tatters. But unlike the other kids, she had plenty of fight left in her.

'I knew you'd come! I knew when Kevin turned up in my dream.'

Kevin went red. 'You saw me in *your* dream?'

All around them, slaves were downing their tools, wondering what was going on.

'I've tried persuading them to escape,' Clare sighed. 'But the guards have got them all terrified.'

'About those guards –' Kevin began.

'It's OK. They've just done their rounds. You should be safe for a bit.'

'All the same, it's gone very quiet in here,' Kevin said uneasily. 'It might be an idea to keep those chains moving.'

The slaves began clanking obediently.

'So what's the plan?' asked Clare.

Flora's face fell. 'Sorry, Clare. We're doing everything we can, honestly. But we can't take you with us just yet.'

Clare made a swift recovery. 'That's OK. If Alice is on

the case, that's good enough for me.' At that moment, Joe knew Flora had been right to trust Clare. She's a real Afterdark kid, like us, he thought.

'Is that magic princess really real then?' interrupted a little boy, his eyes huge with excitement. 'Clare tells us stories about her every night. But my brother says she isn't real.'

'Shut *up*, Colin,' hissed an older boy.

Flora smiled. 'Tell your big brother he's wrong. Alice is one of the most real people you'll ever meet. If everything works out, I promise you'll get to meet her.'

Colin's mouth fell open. 'Will I?'

'Where are Alice and Vasco anyway?' asked Clare.

'They're not allowed in,' Joe explained. 'And somehow we've got to get back to them without those ghouls seeing us. It's probably best to wait till it gets dark.'

Clare shuddered. 'Then you'll wait for ever.'

They stared at her in bewilderment.

She gave an edgy laugh. 'Haven't you noticed? The sun never sets. It never even changes its position by a fraction. The magician has fixed it so Time is always stuck at midday.'

'You mean the sun scorches down like this for twenty-four hours a day?' Flora sounded appalled.

Clare shrugged philosophically. 'That's one good thing about working in the tunnels. You get out of the glare for a few hours.'

Joe's heart sank. 'So how can we get back without the ghouls seeing us?'

'We'll help,' said Colin's brother unexpectedly.

'Yeah, we'll help, Clare!' chorused several children.

Now Clare's strange friends had turned up, her stories of a magical princess seemed less far-fetched. The children all began talking at once.

'We should kick up a ruckus,' said one boy fiercely. 'That's what we should do. It's a kids' city this, you know! It wasn't ever meant to be a ghouls' city!'

The slaves looked more like normal children now, Joe thought. All they'd needed was a tiny spark of hope.

'Keep it *down*,' Kevin insisted. 'And move those chains, will ya?'

Clare explained that there was a network of tunnels under the city.

'It's like a honeycomb down here. If you keep on down this tunnel for a mile or so, it forks in two. We've just checked that one so there won't be any guards. Take the fork to the east and you'll be heading right away from the city.'

Flora hugged her. 'We'll come back for you all as soon as we can.'

'Tell me something, you kids,' said Kevin suddenly. 'What's this old whatsisname actually look like?'

Several children went pale. A few shook their heads in a kind of dread.

Little Colin put his finger to his lips. 'We can't tell you,' he whispered.

'Why, because he'll be angry?' said Joe.

A small girl shook her head. 'Because we don't know.'

'Nobody ever sees the magician,' said Colin gravely. 'But he sees everybody.'

'Yeah, well his days are numbered, mate.' Kevin took a deep breath. 'Right, is everyone ready to kick up this really big ruckus?' he demanded, like a dame in a pantomime.

'YESSS!' yelled everyone.

Joe, Flora and Kevin crouched behind a pile of fallen rock. The slaves began to rattle their chains, yelling at the tops of their voices.

When the guards appeared, the slave children ran at them, roaring like wild animals. 'Go away! Go away! This is our city now!'

They knew they were going to be punished, Joe thought. They were total heroes. He had to force himself not to stay to see what happened next. They fled along the tunnel, the sounds of uproar fading behind them.

'I hope they'll be OK,' he said.

Flora sounded tearful. 'Clare is so brave.'

By this time they were in total darkness. 'We haven't got Alice's torch,' Joe remembered.

Kevin's voice was calm. 'No problem! Flora will be

our loyal seeing-eye vampire, won't you?'

'Ha ha,' said Flora.

Even with Flora's help, slogging down a tunnel in pitch darkness was tough going. The tunnel seemed to go on for ever.

Then just as Joe thought he couldn't go any further, he saw a ray of light, like a far-off star. At first he thought he was seeing daylight. Then he realised the light was coming steadily towards them, growing brighter and clearer with every second. And all at once Joe smelled the sweet, familiar fragrance of the Afterdark princess.

Alice and Vasco had come to find them!

The children ran into their arms, all talking at once.

'We're so sorry,' blurted Flora.

'We shouldn't have run off,' said Joe.

'You're safe, that's the main thing,' said Alice.

Vasco sounded admiring. 'How did you manage to get past the guards?'

Flora explained how Clare and the others had helped them.

'We found those symbols,' said Kevin. 'Got them stored in here.' He tapped his forehead.

'Then we must get you all home pronto,' said Vasco. 'Once the magician knows you've beaten him to the symbols –'

'We'll be toast,' said Kevin cheerfully.

Everyone agreed that it would be safer for the children to

figure out the symbols in their own world.

Vasco insisted on coming with them as far as the Ivory Gates.

For the first few miles the journey was uneventful. Then suddenly, a beautiful little oasis materialised out of the shimmering air.

'Not again,' growled Kevin.

Luckily Flora didn't hear him. 'Oh, it's so cute,' she gasped. 'I've never seen a mirage!'

'There's nothing to them, believe me,' said Joe in a weary voice. 'Ignore it. It'll go away in a minute.'

But Vasco was enchanted. 'I don't want it to go anywhere. I want to move in permanently!'

Kevin grinned. 'You've had too much sun, mate.'

The mirage could have been an identical twin to the first; the same Arabian Nights tent, the same languid camel under the palm trees. Only this time someone had hung some glamorous clothes out to dry.

'Who do they belong to?' marvelled Flora. 'A film star?'

Suddenly there was a breathtaking burst of tiny coloured stars.

'*Moi*,' said a little husky voice. Everyone gasped.

'*They belong to little ole ME!*' giggled the invisible someone.

'Who ARE you?' asked Flora.

'*Who am I? What am I?*' sang the voice cheekily.

'*If you'd really like to know,*

Please let me entertain you
With my mirage magic show!'

Vasco burst out laughing. 'At least tell us what you look like!'

'I'm glossy and glitzy,'
the voice sang back.

'I'm always brand new,
And if you loved me in sequins
You'll ADORE me in blue!'

The invisible creature seemed to be jumping around crazily. Either that or it was an expert ventriloquist. Each time they thought they'd tracked it down, a starburst went up somewhere completely different.

'OK, *what* are you?' giggled Flora. 'A jumping bean? A flea circus?'

'Sounds like a right fashion victim, whoever it is,' muttered Kevin.

'I'm always in fashion,
But I'm not in your face,'
sang the voice immediately.

'So why is it we can't see you?' asked Alice.

'I blend in. I'm discreet.
I've got TASTE!'
shouted the voice triumphantly.

By this time almost everyone was dancing crazily in and out of the drying clothes, searching for the mysterious singer. Even Alice was acting all giggly. Kevin was clowning, peering at Flora through a gauzy gown. Somehow this creature had drawn them all into its game.

'*I'm the king of disguises,*'
it carolled,
'*I'm one step ahead.*
'*Cos if you ever stop changing*
You're basically DEAD!'

'Well, that's true,' grinned Vasco.

Flora tried to pull Joe into the dance. 'Don't be a party pooper.'

He shook his head. He was listening intently to the words of the riddle. Beneath the fun and fireworks, he alone sensed the faintest of threats.

'Last verse coming up!' announced the voice, and Joe thought it sounded oddly triumphant.

'*I'm the softness on velvet.*
I'm the shine on a star . . .'

In a flash, Joe had the answer. 'You're a chameleon!'

And there, posing on the washing line, like a tightrope walker, was the largest and certainly the strangest lizard Joe had ever seen.

'What do you know!' chortled Vasco. 'An all-singing, all-dancing chameleon!'

The lizard flicked out a lazy tongue. 'Glad you enjoyed the show,' it drawled.

The game was over. With a final starburst, the mirage, with its ritzy laundry and its chameleon magic show, vanished like a dream.

For the rest of the journey everyone was unusually subdued.

The chameleon's boastful words kept going round Joe's brain. '*I'm the king of disguises, I'm one step ahead . . .*' That lizard made fools of us, Joe thought uneasily. Like the bubble bath girl. It's like he deliberately wanted to make us look stupid. But why?

Dusk was falling as they reached the ivory gates.

'GATES!' Vasco roared to the trolls on the other side. The trolls came lumbering up. But Vasco didn't move. 'I'll wait till you're safely inside, if you don't mind,' he said quietly.

Alice pulled a face. 'Vee! How do you think I manage when you're not around?' But she threw her arms around him. 'Just don't get too attached to that ghoul outfit.'

They watched from the other side of the gates as Vasco's lonely figure hurried away into the desert.

Then Joe registered something extremely disturbing.

Darkness was falling all around them. Yet on the horizon, he could see a distant flare of light. Daylight.

Flora saw his expression. 'Clare says it's one of her worst things.' She shook her head. 'And I just walked off and left her.'

'You couldn't exactly take her and leave the others,' Kevin pointed out. 'Besides, if you ask me, it's only Clare that's keeping those kids going.'

Joe tried to imagine Clare's existence as a slave. No dusks, no dawns, no rain or rest. Just working endlessly under a harsh unchanging sun.

'Yeah, but now I've seen it, I can't pretend I don't know,' Flora explained shakily.

'None of us can,' said Joe.

His sister looked sick with horror.

'You heard what Clare said,' she whispered. 'He's fixed it so Time is permanently stuck at midday. It's always noon, Joe. Never-ending noon.'

8
Vampire moods

They were back on the right side of the mirror, in the Midnight Museum. Joe could never get over how slowly real-world time moved, compared with the Afterdark kind. They'd been away for ages, yet here it was still only Saturday afternoon.

'Alice,' said Flora anxiously. 'What if we picked the wrong symbols?'

'If you listened to your hearts, you chose right,' Alice reassured her.

Kevin puffed out his cheeks. 'How can you tell? How do you know you're not kidding yourself?'

Alice took a breath. 'I never told you this before,' she said. 'I suppose I didn't want you to get the wrong idea.'

Flora swallowed. 'This sounds a bit scary.'

Alice took another deep breath. 'I've been training you for this task since the day we met.'

Joe felt oddly betrayed. 'Training us?' he said angrily. 'I thought we were just having fun.'

She made him look at her. 'No, you didn't.'

'No. I didn't.'

Alice's eyes sparkled. 'And we did have fun, didn't we? But the magician's city affected you more than you know. Go home and get some sleep.'

The going home part was easy. Sleep was more of a problem.

That night, Joe's bedroom door creaked open. 'Flora?' he hissed. 'Are you OK?'

'Fine. Why, did I wake you?'

'Just dozing,' he said.

He switched on his lamp. His sister had a pile of battered boxes under her arm, board games she'd had for years.

Her voice sounded very small. 'I've got this stupid tummy ache. Can we play a game, till it goes off?'

'Sure.'

'Is Snakes and Ladders OK?'

They propped the board on the bed between them.

Flora shook the dice in its little plastic cup. 'I couldn't stop thinking,' she said sheepishly. 'And games are so restful. Almost as good as maths.'

Flora adored anything with rules. Joe tended to forget it was just a game, taking each setback personally. After he'd won one game and Flora won three, his sister rubbed her eyes. 'I'm going back to bed now.'

'OK.'

She switched off his light. 'Thanks, Joe. Mind the bugs don't bite.'

'You too.'

And she was gone.

Before Joe knew it, sunlight was pouring in through his curtains and it was morning. That wasn't so bad, he thought. No bad dreams. No dreams, full stop!

Joe threw on his clothes and went downstairs.

In the kitchen, Flora was absently picking freeze-dried raspberries out of her cereal, while she read the cartoon section of the Sunday papers. She went into fits of laughter. 'That is SO funny!' she said.

'Did you sleep OK?'

His sister's smile vanished. 'That's a funny question,' she snapped.

'No need to bite my head off.' He lowered his voice. 'Hey, maybe today we'll figure out what those weird symbols are for.'

Flora had gone back to reading her cartoons.

'The symbols,' Joe repeated. 'Hope we crack them today.'

But Flora was laughing so hard she couldn't hear him.

Tom came in, with Tat in his arms. 'Hello, sleepy-heads,' he chuckled. 'Isn't it a wonderful morning? Let's treat ourselves and have a great day out together.'

'Can we afford it?' asked Joe anxiously.

'Can we *afford* it?' Tom echoed. He ruffled Joe's head. 'Since when was money more important than this family?' he beamed.

Joe beamed back. 'Well, if you put it like that,' he agreed.

Flora held out her arms. 'Let me have her. Oooh! She's such a yummy bunny! Yes, you *are!*'

Tat snuggled up to her big sister.

In her efforts to turn her stepdaughter into a normal toddler, Joe's mum had given her two cute little paint-brush bunches. In her rosy pink dungarees with their alphabet pattern, Tat did look almost edibly sweet. For once she didn't even try to bite.

Hang on, thought Joe suspiciously. This is like having breakfast with the Waltons!

He dashed over to the kitchen window. But the morning sky was completely moon-free.

Flora came over, cuddling Tat. 'What are you looking at?' she asked.

He pulled a face. 'Don't laugh. I had a major panic attack. I thought this was all a dream. But obviously the moon's not there, which makes me prize wally of the year.'

Flora burst into peals of laughter. 'Joe, you are such a worry-wart. You should get out more. I know! Let's go to the park for a while, and try out Dad's new frisbee.'

Joe was astonished. For one thing he had no idea Tom

even owned a frisbee. For another, Flora and fresh air didn't exactly go together.

'We promised Alice we'd figure out our symbols,' he reminded her.

Flora's face darkened. 'Will you stop making such a big deal about those stupid symbols! It won't kill Alice to wait for once. Why can't we ever have fun like normal children?'

'Don't be like that, Flo,' he pleaded.

'It's not me that's being a party pooper. I got up in a great mood. All I wanted was to go to the park with my new brother.'

Joe stared at her. 'But Clare and the others are depending on us.'

Flora's eyes blazed. 'Joe Quail, you are such a loser,' she spat, and scraping back her chair, she stormed out of the room.

Joe was shaken. He'd grown used to what he thought of as Flora's 'vampire moods', but this was something else.

I need to talk to Kevin, he thought.

He grabbed his jacket. 'Just popping out for a bit,' he yelled to Tom.

Joe arrived outside Kevin's house just as his friend came jogging out into the street, wearing a smart new football strip. 'Hey, my man!' called Kevin. 'What's up?'

'Good question,' said Joe miserably. 'Flora's acting really strange. You don't think You Know Who might have —'

Kevin interrupted him. 'Love to stay and chat, mate,' he said breezily. 'But they're expecting me up at the school. We've got a match, remember? I'm playing with the first team.'

'Oh, right,' said Joe. It looked as if he'd have to cope all by himself. 'Well, good luck,' he said unhappily.

Kevin seemed to have a sudden brainwave. 'There's no chance you could help us out, is there? Our star striker's ill, and we can't find a replacement. What do you say?'

'You are kidding!'

'Why do you always put yourself down? I've seen you kicking a ball around, remember? I was impressed, Joe. So were the guys in the team. I don't know where you got this idea you're rubbish at games. You've got class, mate.'

Joe couldn't believe this was actually happening. It was his all-time top-favourite daydream! A glow of happiness spread through his body. 'Well, if you really mean it.'

Kevin punched the air. 'You've only saved our lives, Joe! You're only like the hero of the hour, that's all!' He slung a brotherly arm around Joe's shoulders. They moved off down the street, still chatting.

But after a few minutes, Joe felt uneasy. It took next to no time to walk down their road as a rule. But today the pavement stretched on for miles. Also the sun seemed unnaturally bright. Joe began to feel hot. There was something wrong about all of this, but he couldn't think what.

'Erm, Kevin, I'm going to have to let you down,' he said anxiously. 'I've just remembered, Tom's taking us all out for the day.'

But Kevin just stared ahead with an oddly fixed expression, and kept on walking. His grip had become unpleasantly tight.

'Cut it out, Kev!' said Joe. But Kevin didn't answer.

And suddenly Joe knew what was wrong. I mustn't panic, he thought wildly. I must stay calm. I've just got to find the marker, then I'll wake up inside my dream and everything will be OK.

He strained against the dead weight of Kevin's arm. 'I want to see the moon,' he yelled ridiculously.

With a mighty effort, Joe succeeded in lifting his head.

But there was no moon in the colourless sky, only the mocking white disc of the sun.

Through a blur of panic, Joe saw they were heading for the park.

A hot wind began to blow, bringing stinging clouds of dust and the cries of frightened children. How will I save them now, he thought despairingly, when I can't even save myself?

And he walked numbly through the gates and out the other side.

The park had gone. In its place, sand dunes rippled to the horizon like a shimmering inland sea. In the distance was a vast jumble of sun-bleached stone.

With a feeling of horrible inevitability, Joe forced himself to look at Kevin. It wasn't Kevin, of course. Just as Flora hadn't really been Flora.

Looming over him, grinning emptily, was the figure he most dreaded to see: the magician's ghoul, which had tricked Joe into slavery, trapping him in the ruined city for ever.

9

The wrong kind of magic

Flora knew something was wrong the minute she opened her eyes.

She tried to sit up and fell back with a groan. Her head felt as if it was full of hot sawdust. Even her skin hurt.

She recognised her symptoms immediately. Afterdark vampires have delicate nervous systems. Flora's had been exposed to the wrong kind of magic, and she was suffering the consequences.

Her own mother would have known exactly what to do. But if Flora described her aches and pains to Joe's mum, she'd just dose her with Lemsip and send her back to bed.

Needing comfort, Flora felt for the storm-stone around her neck. She kept it on night and day. She'd tried taking it off once or twice, but quickly missed its tingling presence against her skin.

I'll keep you safe, the stone seemed to whisper.

A flash of fear went through her. She'd been awake

almost ten minutes and she hadn't checked the sky! Flora tottered over to the window and gave a huge sigh of relief.

Not only was there no moon, there was no sun either. The sky was dull and cloudy. Just another boring Sunday, thank goodness, she thought.

On her way to the bathroom, Flora noticed Joe's door was still closed.

He's probably shattered, she thought. He'd been such a star, sitting up playing games, until she felt able to go to sleep.

Flora felt better after her shower. If she didn't move her head too fast, she could convince herself she felt normal. She couldn't afford to lose her edge, today of all days. They had to crack those magical symbols, and get Clare and the others out of that nightmarish city.

Flora threw on her oldest, most comfortable clothes. On the way down to breakfast, she glanced at Joe's door. It was still shut.

She heard Joe's mum in the kitchen, sounding slightly desperate. 'You don't want to hurt your nice dolly, do you, Titania?'

'Yesh,' said Tat huskily. 'Hurt my mice dolly.'

Flora sighed. Tat was the kind of child who gave vampires a bad name.

When Tat saw Flora, she dropped the doll she was

torturing, and held up her arms for a hug.

'Erm, where's Dad?' Flora asked. The idea of spending any time alone with Geraldine Quail still made her incredibly jumpy.

'He's getting in some writing time while it's quiet,' said Joe's mum. 'Quite a good sign, don't you think?'

'That depends,' said Flora cautiously.

Joe's mother raised her eyebrows.

'Is it actual writing time, or just staring at his computer in a blind panic time?'

Geraldine Quail gave a startled giggle. 'A bit of both, I should think!'

There was a loud SNAP! and Betty Einstein shot in through her catflap. She looked even more demented than usual. Her ears lay flat against her skull, and her yellow eyes seemed wild with terror.

Geraldine sighed. 'Must be a full moon. She only went out sixty seconds ago!'

Flora went to stroke her. 'What's up, cat?'

Betty Einstein skidded past her into the hall, and they heard paws thundering up the stairs.

'I question that animal's sanity,' said Joe's mum. She gave a little cough. 'I'm taking Tat to the swings. I could wait till you've had breakfast, if you wanted to come?'

'Oh, thanks, Geraldine,' said Flora in her politest voice. 'But I've got this stupid project.'

Her stepmother looked wistful. 'This must be some project. It's taken you all weekend.'

Flora tried to smile. 'You have no idea.'

After breakfast, she sat leafing through the cartoon section of the Sunday papers, waiting for Joe to come downstairs. Meanwhile, still under the influence of her own private full moon, Betty Einstein continued to charge around the house as if the hounds of hell were after her.

All at once, Flora ran out of patience. Joe can laze around all day if he likes, she thought. She took a note-pad and crayons into the sitting room, and began reconstructing her symbol from memory.

When it was finished, Flora stared at her artwork, willing it to give up its magical secrets. It looks a bit like a flame, she thought. But only a bit. 'Concentrate, Flora,' she muttered.

She heard the sound of a key in the lock. Geraldine was back with Tat.

'Don't tell me that boy is still snoring upstairs,' she joked. 'I'd better wake him, if he's got this project to do.' She sped upstairs. 'Want some coffee, Tom?' she called cheerfully.

Tat squatted down to inspect Flora's drawing, and blew on her fingers. 'Ouch. Careful! Might burn yourself.'

Flora giggled. 'You clever girl.'

Then Joe's mother screamed.

The blood drained from Flora's face. She tore upstairs. A

frantic Betty Einstein overtook her on the bend.

'He won't wake up!' Geraldine wept.

Betty Einstein jumped on to the bed and began kneading Joe's chest with her hard little paws, making the anxious 'Prrp' sound cats use to warn their kittens away from danger. It was so pitiful, Flora knew it should break her heart. But she only felt numb.

Flora tried to tell her parents it was pointless trying to wake Joe, but they thought she was just babbling hysterically. 'You're not making sense, sweetheart,' said Tom.

She was forced to stand by and watch as their efforts became increasingly distraught. At last they called an ambulance. It came, its blue lights flashing, and took Joe and his mother to the hospital. Tom followed in the car with Tat.

'Phone as soon as you have any news,' Flora called from the doorway, as if she actually believed the doctors could do Joe any good. 'This isn't happening,' she whispered to herself.

And for fifty glorious seconds, Flora succeeded in convincing herself that it was all a dream. It wasn't Joe who was in the magician's clutches, but Flora, dream expert and vampire supersleuth. Then horror welled up inside her and she knew her nightmare was real.

He should have taken me, she thought bitterly. I can defend myself.

Now that her numbness was wearing off, Flora discovered that she was not just upset. She was also hopping mad.

She picked up the phone and punched out Kevin's number. While she waited for him to answer, she furiously traced and retraced her symbol, until the tiny flame resembled a raging bonfire.

Kevin came at once, looking deathly pale. 'I saw the ambulance, but I never thought –' He couldn't finish the sentence. 'We'll never rescue those kids now,' he said at last. 'We're done for.'

'You give up easily,' jeered Flora.

Kevin looked stung. 'No, I don't.'

'Then stop whingeing! We're going over to the museum in a minute, and I don't want Alice to see a pair of losers.'

'Hey, thanks, Flora,' muttered Kevin.

But Flora couldn't afford to be kind. She had to be strong for Joe. She hurtled on, ignoring Kevin's hurt feelings.

'This is what we're going to do,' she said, in her bossiest voice. 'You, me and Alice will put our heads together, and figure out those symbols. Then we'll go bombing back to Afterdark and we'll blow that magician's socks off, OK?'

'Mmn, nice plan! Assuming you know what symbol Joe actually picked? Showed it to his big sister before he went off to beddy-byes, did he?'

Flora stopped breathing. Then she swooped on her

drawing and ripped it angrily into shreds. 'Aaargh!' she yelled. 'I'm so *stupid!*

'Oops,' murmured Kevin. 'He didn't, right?'

Tears spilled down Flora's face. 'I should have made us draw them the minute we got back,' she choked.

'OK, maybe you should. Then again, maybe you shouldn't. *Someone* might have been spying on us, with his evil little magician's eye, and got *us* to solve his puzzle for him, instead of his slaves.'

But Flora had stopped listening. 'It's OK, Kevin. I know what we're going to do.'

Kevin sounded weary. 'You reckon?'

She stared fiercely at him through her tears.

'It's simple. Before we can destroy the magician, we've got to rescue Joe!'

10

The pyramid
chain-gang

Joe was not the only child who was captured that night. He counted fifty new slaves being herded through the ruins by their empty-eyed guards.

With signs and gestures, the ghouls forbade them to speak. From time to time scared whimpers escaped from the younger ones.

All the slave children had that flickery TV look, including Joe himself.

It gave him the heebie-jeebies at first, like seeing his own ghost. Then he gave himself a fierce talking-to. He was the same person inside, no matter what creepy stunts the magician pulled.

As the ghouls drove their ghostly flock through the ruined streets, Joe tried to imagine the city as it had been, long long ago.

There would have been colours, not this endless sun-bleached sand and stone. There would have been trees and fountains, and wonderful statues. And instead of subdued shuffling sounds as they tramped through the dust, you'd hear birdsong and wind-chimes and happy sounds of celebration.

Joe surfaced abruptly from his daydream as their guards brought them to a halt in what was once a city square. This rest was not for the children's benefit, however, but the magician's.

There was a livid flash and heavy chains went snaking around their ankles. Everyone cried out in dismay at this dark magic.

With signs and proddings, the ghouls urged them on.

This time, Joe was chained to nine other slaves. They stumbled along in the dust for what seemed endless miles. Joe wasn't physically exhausted as he would have been in waking life, but he felt battered by despair.

At last they reached their destination: the crumbling remains of a massive pyramid.

Slaves were sifting and tapping little fragments of ancient stone and marble. They had the hopeless air Joe had noticed on his first visit. And now Joe was one of them.

The new slaves were instantly put to work moving rocks.

Joe decided the magician had finally gone off his head. Why inflict all this suffering, just to cart rocks aimlessly from place to place?

Working in chains was tough going. You had to find a

rhythm of bending and lifting which didn't involve crashing into your fellow slaves.

Then a boy's voice rang out, 'Can't tell if it's dusk or dawn . . .' He sang the words like a question which needed a response.

There was a pause. 'Can't tell if it's dusk or dawn . . .' the voice repeated hopefully.

To his surprise, Joe sang back. 'Could have been here since I was born!'

'Can't tell if it's three or six,' sang the invisible singer immediately.

' 'Cos of these stupid magic tricks,' yelled Joe.

Some of the slaves looked nervous, but a few giggled.

'Sticks and stones can't hurt my bones,' the boy added.

'Had to leave my bones at home,' sang a girl.

'Pyramid slave kids sang this song,' replied the boy.

'Hope we don't have to sing too long!' Joe joined in.

The tune was so catchy that soon everyone was singing as they worked, even those who didn't understand the words. And suddenly Joe found his rhythm, though he never saw the boy who sang to him.

Now Joe was able to lift his head occasionally to sneak a look around.

Slowly and painfully, the slaves were unblocking what had been a grand and forbidding entrance.

On either side stood a statue of a giant cat. Joe supposed

they had been identical once, but centuries of sandstorms had battered them so badly that one only had a sightless stump for a head.

The remaining cat seemed oddly familiar. At first Joe thought he was remembering that never-ending Egyptian project he'd done at his old primary school. Then he realised it was the spitting image of Betty Einstein in her most snooty mood.

A wave of homesickness washed over him. Joe shut his eyes, swallowing. He could smell her fur. For someone who spent so much time batting dead mice about, Betty Einstein's fur smelled surprisingly nice.

Once, when Joe had a temperature, the little cat had crept into his room and curled up on his pillow. She'd purred so loudly, it seemed she'd taken it upon herself to purr him back to health. Joe had been so grateful, he hadn't even minded her hooky claws jabbing rhythmically in and out of his neck.

It was a terribly lonely feeling, knowing that the real world of cats and school was carrying on without him. Visiting a magic world through choice was one thing. Being taken there by force was quite another.

It's my own fault, he thought. I can't believe I fell for that football thing. That magician must be laughing himself sick.

He became aware of frantic sniffing sounds and realised that the little boy beside him was struggling not to cry.

'Hey,' Joe teased. 'Just because we can't see the pattern in the stars, doesn't mean it isn't there, you know.'

All the chain-gang kids gave Joe blank stares. He grinned sheepishly. 'I didn't get it either,' he admitted. 'But when Spinner says it, it's pure magic!'

Then a hooded shape loomed between Joe and the sun, and everyone hastily went back to work.

But as the hours crawled by Joe lost heart. The evil in the magician's city seemed to be sucking all the hope out of him.

He'd find himself staring at a pile of rocks, without a clue what he was meant to be doing. It felt as if he'd been working under this glaring sun for ever. Think positive, he told himself bravely. At this very moment, Vasco and everyone are probably galloping to our rescue on a herd of wild camels!

But he could not have predicted what actually happened next in a million years.

A strange fluting cry rang around the pyramid. It sent a flash of excitement through Joe, as if he'd heard it before, long ago.

There it was again, but closer. The slaves cowered, fearing some new magical threat, but Joe stared around him eagerly. What could possibly be making such wonderful sounds? It definitely wasn't a ghoul. It was real, though possibly not human.

Soft as a thief, something landed beside him. 'You are Joe Quail, yes?' said a voice.

For two seconds, Joe truly believed he was gawping at some raggedy desert bird with the power of human speech. Then his heart gave a thump of fear. At the worst possible moment, Joe had finally run into one of Spinner's blood-thirsty bird-people.

Dozens of bird-warriors came swarming down into the pyramid, seeming to defy gravity with their speed and agility.

They looked terrifying in their war-paint and bizarre feathery tunics, but appeared unusually small for warriors. Then Joe understood. They were children!

The warriors whipped out glittering knives and spears, calling to each other constantly in a strange and wonderful language.

'Joe Quail, yes?' the first warrior, a girl, repeated impatiently.

'Yes,' he croaked. 'I'm Joe.'

'Ha! I have found you!' With a deafening war-whoop, she raised her spear above her head.

Joe closed his eyes and prepared to die. The air filled with the horrific sound of metal battering metal. Behind his eyelids, Joe glimpsed white sparks, and felt a brief searing heat.

Surprisingly, there was no pain. He opened his eyes warily.

Whooping with triumph, the bird-girl held up a length of useless chain, then tossed it away with contempt. For reasons Joe could only guess at, she had set him free!

'What about the others?' he cried.

'That is for another day,' she yelled. 'You must come with us!'

The ghouls had come running, but the bird-children fought them off fearlessly. With a rush of exhilaration, Joe joined in, getting in a couple of lucky hits with Spinner's sling-shot.

At last they hurried him away, urging him over walls, across broken rooftops and down sudden sickening drops, all at tremendous speed.

Joe was so stunned at his miraculous escape, he wouldn't have been more surprised if the children had sprouted wings and swept him up into the air.

They soon left the city behind, and began to head up into the hills.

All this time, the girl had stuck close to his side. At one point, they had fought the ghouls back-to-back and Joe thought it was time he knew her name. But when he gasped out his question she snapped, 'Save your breath to climb!' Her expression changed. 'You are very happy now, Joe Quail. But do not think you are free.'

He felt a prickle of horror. 'What do you mean?'

Her dark eyes glittered through her war-paint. 'You will

never see your loved ones again, unless –' she stopped.

'Unless,' he prompted shakily.

'You must fight the sorcerer, Joe Quail. You must fight.
And you must win.'

11
Flora fights back

'Map, torch, knife,' Kevin murmured. 'Snake whatsisname.'

He was checking their kit while Alice anxiously ran-sacked her library, looking for advice on outwitting magicians.

'Ow!' said Flora. She dragged off her boot and peered inside. 'I don't believe it! There's still sand in here from last time!'

Alice replaced a book on the shelf. 'Huh,' she snorted. 'That nitwit wouldn't recognise an evil sorcerer if it poked him in the eye. Oh, don't forget to pack Flora's remedy.'

Kevin saluted. 'Yes ma'am!'

Alice felt Flora's forehead. 'How are you feeling?'

'Better, thanks. Let's go!'

Alice shook her head. 'You do know we can't just rush off? What happened to Joe didn't just affect your world. It would be disrespectful to do anything without asking my grandfather's permission first.'

Flora's face fell. 'What if he says no?'

'Alice said we had to *ask*,' Kevin grinned. 'She didn't say we'd do what he tells us.'

Flora suddenly clutched at Alice's sleeve. 'We will save Joe, won't we?'

'Yes,' Alice told her fiercely.

She touched her palm to the mirror. For a third time, the glass grew bright and fluid and they crossed effortlessly into Alice's kingdom.

Flora was startled to find herself outdoors, under a glittering night sky. There was a strong smell of wood smoke from the camp-fires dotted around in the dark. Horses stamped and whinnied restlessly.

The warrior's camp had doubled in size since their last visit. New arrivals were hastily putting up tents and queuing for rations. Everyone seemed grim and preoccupied.

The ivory gates looked more ominous than ever by night, gleaming with their own eerie moonlight, and casting such disturbing shadows on the watchful faces of the trolls that Flora had to look away.

Suddenly she caught sight of a beautiful little pavilion. Black and silver pennants fluttered in the night air. Four troll guards barred the entrance.

Flora felt a flicker of unease. *That's* why the magic brought us to the camp, she thought. The king and queen aren't at the court at all. They're here.

'Things are worse than I thought,' Alice muttered. With

an unusually set expression, she went marching towards the pavilion. Flora and Kevin hurried after her.

'What's going on?' Flora whispered.

'Looks like they've given up on the prophecy,' hissed Kevin out of the side of his mouth. 'They're getting ready to go to war.'

The princess marched straight up to the astonished guards, who immediately stood aside.

The children followed her nervously into the royal pavilion.

The king and queen were at a long table with their advisers. A heated argument was going on.

'We are running out of time, your majesties,' someone was saying. 'If you delay, it will be seen as a weakness on your part. We must act before it's too late.' The speaker was an improbably young general, and like most vampires he was extremely good-looking. But Flora thought his caring smile looked about as convincing as a glued-on moustache.

'But the prophecy, General Snipe,' began the queen.

An adviser with a nose like a ripe strawberry made tisking sounds. 'With the greatest respect,' he said impatiently. 'This is not a fairytale. We can't just hope these unknown children will produce our happy ending, like conjurers. The magician has the boy and that changes everything.'

'Exactly,' Snipe agreed. 'Therefore I urge your majesties to send in the troops. We must destroy what remains of that unhappy city and purge it of its unsavoury inhabitants.'

There was an uncomfortable silence during which everyone suddenly noticed Alice and the children.

'Alice, my dear,' said the king hastily. 'What an unexpected surprise. Come and join us.'

But Alice didn't move.

'Your highness,' Snipe smirked. 'May I say how well you're looking?'

Kevin's lip curled. 'Sorry to interrupt your important meeting and everything. But when the general here says "purge", he means "kill", right?'

The advisers made embarrassed noises.

Flora was horrified. 'He can't do that! What about Joe? What about Clare and all those other children?'

'My dear, they are no longer children in any real sense,' said a female vampire. 'Theirs is a twilight existence, barely half-alive.'

'And there is absolutely no guarantee they could ever be returned to their normal condition,' said the adviser with the strawberry nose.

Flora felt a sob rising up in her throat. 'But you asked us to save them,' she whispered. 'It was in the prophecy.'

'It is regrettable of course,' agreed Snipe. 'But —'

'It is not regrettable. It is terrible,' the queen corrected him icily. 'At least let us call things by their right names.'

'Yes, yes, it is terrible, ma'am. But these are terrible times, as I'm sure you agree.' Snipe's voice was as smooth as cream. 'And to save the many in our kingdom, it is necessary to sacrifice the few —'

Suddenly Flora didn't care how important these people were. 'Don't even talk about it!' she yelled. 'Because it's not going to happen. We're going to get my brother back, and we're going to rescue Clare, and we're going to destroy the magician like it says in that prophecy. And all those kids will go safely home to their families. *End of story!*'

Snipe's eyes glittered. 'Sorry, my dear, could you just remind me. Are you half-vampire, or is it only one-quarter?'

'You're being a bit personal!' said Kevin angrily. 'Why do you need to know that?'

Snipe looked amused. 'It's just that with Flora's background being so, erm, *colourful*, it's hardly surprising her loyalties get confused. Naturally she's more worried about her father's people than about the catastrophic impact of an all-powerful magician on her mother's world.'

Flora felt as if the vampire had slapped her. It was the cruellest thing anyone had ever said to her.

Kevin scowled, but before he could spring to Flora's defence, Alice drew a furious breath. 'How dare you insult one of Afterdark's most loyal friends.'

General Snipe opened his mouth, but the queen gave him such a steely glare that he hastily closed it again.

'It's easy to be a vampire, when you live among vampires,'

said Alice. 'Flora has to make her way without any guidance from her people. It is a long and lonely path, and she shows as much courage as any warrior here tonight.'

The princess spoke so passionately that Flora's eyes prickled with tears. Alice took a step towards the king. 'I am begging you not to invade the city, grandfather,' she said quietly. 'We can defeat the magician. I'm sure of it. All we need is a little more time.'

'Hear, hear!' said the queen. 'Perhaps by now that enterprising young Vasco has uncovered new clues to the city's secrets.'

Flora got the feeling the queen was quite fond of Vasco.

The king looked uneasy. 'But suppose the magician catches you, too?'

'That's a risk we have to take,' said Alice and Flora simultaneously.

They grinned and shook little fingers. 'Jinx!' they cried.

'This is madness, your majesty,' fumed Snipe. 'If the magician has the boy, he is sure to have his magic symbol by now.'

Kevin did his famous shark's grin. 'Of course, I'm not a big general, like you,' he said slyly. 'But personally, I wouldn't fancy going against an ancient prophecy. But then that's just me, know what I mean?'

The argument continued through the night. But deep down, Flora knew they had already won. Finally the king gave permission for the children to make one last attempt to fulfil the prophecy. 'Seven days,' he told them reluctantly. 'You have seven days and no more.'

They emerged from the pavilion just before sunrise. Faint streaks of rose and aquamarine coloured the sky. They hurried across to the ivory gates, leaving tracks in the dew.

The shivering trolls jumped to attention.

Slowly and laboriously, the gates were dragged back, and for a second time Alice and the children slipped through into the badlands.

At first, the going seemed easier. The sun was still low in the sky, and a pearly mist softened the harshness of the desert landscape.

But as the hours passed, Flora began to find it hard to breathe.

Soon, despite frequent sips of Alice's extremely unpleasant remedy, everyone was feeling ill. By the time they came within sight of the city, the atmosphere of brooding evil felt thick enough to touch, hanging over the ruins like the shadow of some huge malevolent bird.

Vasco was waiting at the tunnel entrance.

'How does he always *know*?' muttered Kevin. 'Vampire intuition?'

Alice hugged him. 'I'm so glad you're safe.'

Vasco was looking crisp and cool in his tropical suit, in

spite of the searing desert heat. But Flora could tell he was worried.

He quickly confirmed their fears. 'I'm afraid the sorcerer's dangerously close to unlocking the city's secrets.'

'Any news of Joe?' asked Flora.

Vasco looked cagey. 'Actually, yes.'

Kevin's face lit up. 'So where is he?'

'You mean, at this precise moment?' Vasco asked vaguely. 'Well, in theory, I suppose, he *could* be anywhere.'

Flora's heart bumped with fear. 'Something's happened, hasn't it?'

Vasco sighed. 'Have you ever heard of the bird-people?'

'I think Spinner warned Joe about them,' said Kevin. 'They're cannibals who kick their kids out the minute they can fend for themselves, so they'll learn to be vicious like their parents.'

'A band of bird-children swooped on Joe's chain-gang, and carried him off into the hills,' Vasco explained.

Flora gave a little gasp of dismay.

Kevin passed his hand across his face, looking dazed. 'This is not good. We were in with a chance while Joe was still in the city. Now these bird bandits have got him, we don't know if he's even alive.'

'Yes, we do,' Flora snapped. 'He's my brother. I'd know if he was dead.'

'No offence, Flo,' Kevin said in a tired voice. 'But not so

long ago, you didn't even know he was in a magic sleep.'

'I'm telling you, I'd know. And I don't believe a word of this cannibal rubbish, either.'

'I'm glad to hear you sounding so positive,' said Vasco wryly. He produced a crumpled map and spread it in front of them. 'It just so happens that we've got to take a trip through their territory.'

They stared at him.

Vasco jabbed his finger at the map. 'This is where Joe disappeared. The magician is doing some serious excavating here for some reason. Unfortunately, the earthquake created a rather inconvenient abyss between the east, where we are now, and the west, where we want to be.'

'That kind of rules out tunnels then,' said Kevin.

Vasco nodded. 'And using magic would attract unwanted attention. Our best route is across the desert and up into the mountains. You never know, we might run into Joe on the way. As Flora says, those cannibal stories are probably a bit of an exaggeration.'

'You mean those bird bandits are like, only slightly cannibal?' jeered Kevin.

Flora narrowed her eyes. 'I told you, they're not cannibals.'

'How long will it take?' asked Alice.

'Too long,' said Vasco. 'But what choice do we have?'

There was none, and they all knew it.

✳   ✳   ✳

Two days later, Flora was climbing through lush tropical foliage and feeling as if she had entered a completely different world.

Sunlight filtered down through the dense forest canopy, making leaf-patterns dance across her skin. The air was warm and moist, and the trees were filled with the soft fluting cries of birds.

They had spent the night in a cave, an experience Flora hoped she'd never have to repeat. It was Vasco's fault. He would go on about the local spiders. According to him, these cunning monsters deliberately wove poisonous webs at heights where humans would walk into them.

But apart from her spider phobia, Flora felt more relaxed than she had for days. Amongst the dappled shadows of the rain forest, she finally felt safe from the all-seeing eyes of the magician. In a funny way, she felt as if the trees were on their side.

She'd been climbing with Vasco for some time, when he said casually, 'Alice told me about your run-in with Snipe. We were at school together.'

Flora stared at him. 'You're kidding?'

Vasco held up a branch so Flora could duck under it. 'We called him Gnasher, because of that phoney smile of his. He was a nasty piece of work even then.'

Flora sensed Vasco was working up to something.

'People like you and me,' he said suddenly, 'people who

belong to both worlds, we have to make it up as we go along. Every day has to be this big new adventure!'

Flora's smile vanished. 'Sorry,' she said coldly. 'That sounds too much like hard work.'

'I know,' he beamed. 'That's what's so great.'

Flora scowled. 'Really. I mean, I can't tell humans who I am, because they'll be disgusted. And now apparently I'm not vampire enough for the vampires. Just why is that so great, exactly?'

'Because when life gets too easy, it becomes incredibly boring. Have you ever met those people who never had anything go wrong their whole lives?' Vasco rolled his eyes. 'They are just one long yawn.'

Flora gazed at him in astonishment. 'What a load of rubbish. Alice told you to talk to me, didn't she? You were trying to cheer me up.'

Vasco looked sheepish. 'Maybe. But just tell me one thing. If you weren't so scared about not fitting in, where would you *choose* to belong? What would you really *love* to do?'

Flora was stunned into silence. Was it really only fear which stood in her way, she wondered? Because if so, she knew the answer to Vasco's question. One day, when she understood them a little better herself, Flora would like to teach the mysteries of vampire existence to humans.

Her heart began to race. It could never happen. It was

just a stupid, impossible dream. Yet she felt a surge of ridiculous happiness.

She glanced sideways and saw Vasco smiling. On a sudden impulse, she picked a morning glory blossom and presented it to him. 'Thanks,' she said shyly. 'I think!' she added, with a crooked little grin.

They had reached the highest part of their climb. Everyone stopped to rest before a long descent. Without realising it, Flora had started humming to herself.

'You're in a good mood, Flo,' said Kevin.

But she didn't feel ready to share her new discovery just yet. 'It's just so peaceful up here,' she explained hastily.

'Yeah, and you can breathe,' agreed Kevin.

Vasco tucked Flora's morning glory blossom into Alice's hair. He whispered something and Alice blushed.

Somewhere nearby, Flora could hear the insistent piping of a bird. Her new happiness made everything so bright and beautiful she could hardly bear it.

I could maybe tell Joe, she thought suddenly. *He'd* understand.

She closed her eyes as the strangely thrilling sound was taken up in the trees all around them. 'Don't you love those birds?' she said dreamily.

Vasco's voice changed. 'I'm not sure.'

She heard him scramble to his feet, but by then it was too late.

Something whispered through the air, spreading as it fell; its placement judged with such deadly accuracy that Alice didn't even have time to reach for her knife.

Beside her, Kevin struggled furiously against the sticky fibres of the net. But it was useless. They were caught like flies in a web.

12

Joe joins the bird tribe

Night was falling as Joe and his mysterious rescuers reached the bird-children's village. His companions called excitedly into the dark.

'Joe Quail! We found Joe Quail!'

'Welcome to my home,' said the bird-girl.

Joe looked around him in surprise.

There was nothing in this lonely patch of rain forest to show that anyone lived here. No paths or gardens. No cooking smells, or cheerful lamplight. Just trees. Unusually large trees. Some had trunks so thick it would take an entire football team to put their arms around them.

Joe felt a flicker of fear. What if Spinner was right about the bird-children? What if they had staged an elaborate rescue, forcing Joe to trek miles into the mountains, only to kill and eat him there?

He glanced down at his ghostly limbs. Get real, he thought ruefully. You're not exactly a great catch!

At that moment, the air erupted with birdcalls. Children

of all ages tumbled excitedly out of the trees. Tiny lights sprang up like fireflies. Someone began beating a drum. Another child began to chirp a strange little song of welcome. And then Joe understood. The bird-children's village had not been visible, because it was built high in the air!

He gazed in wonder at the fairytale dwellings materialising miraculously above his head.

While he stared into the trees, the smaller bird-children were staring at Joe. A little boy daringly reached out, and went into fits of nervous giggles as his hands plunged through Joe's cloudy trainers. It felt unpleasantly intimate, like being tickled from the inside.

Suddenly the bird-children were all over Joe, experimentally tweaking and patting at his flickery dream body. And as they poked and prodded, they repeated his name excitedly to each other, *Joe Quail, Joe Quail, Joe Quail,* until it sounded as musical and strange as their own birdcalls. They seemed to think Joe was some kind of celebrity.

It was all too much. He felt a strange roaring in his ears. A girl hastily steadied him in her arms, calling loudly for help. The world began to spin around him, and everything went black.

When Joe opened his eyes again, it was almost daylight, and his bed seemed to be rocking gently like a giant cradle.

He struggled upright, and was horrified to discover that

he was several hundred metres off the ground. He had apparently spent the night in one of the bird-children's aerial dwellings.

Someone had wrapped him in a snug, if ticklish, quilt of many-coloured feathers.

The sun was rising and the forest rang with liquid cries. Joe couldn't yet distinguish between actual birdcalls and the fluting sounds of the bird-children.

'You are awake!' said a shy voice.

Joe jumped with fright. He had completely failed to see the little girl among the leaves. She couldn't be more than six or seven years old.

She giggled. 'We took turns to watch you. First Silk, next Wishbone, then me. My name is Fade, because I'm the best at hiding.'

'Was it Silk who rescued me?' he asked.

Fade nodded. 'This is her house. You like guava?' she asked suddenly. Without waiting for his reply, she split a lumpy green fruit down the middle, offering him half. She squatted beside him, her tribal beads chinking musically, and showed Joe how to remove the tiny blue-black seeds from the peach-coloured flesh.

He grinned. 'They'd never recognise me at home.'

She broke into a sweet smile, and Joe saw she had lost one of her baby teeth. 'But *I* recognise you, Joe Quail,' she confided.

Joe was baffled. 'How could you? You never saw me before.'

'From the pictures in here,' she said gravely. She tapped her head.

Joe stared at her. 'You dreamed about me?'

She giggled, covering her mouth. 'Not just me, crazy boy! All bird-children had this dream. That's how we knew it was sent by our ancestors, and that's why we came to find you.'

'And your dream told you my name?'

'No, the trees told us,' she said calmly.

Joe stared. 'You're actually telling me the trees knew my name?'

'Of course. Trees know everything.'

Joe was lost for words. They sat silently eating their fruit, listening to the sounds of the forest. A tiny white-faced monkey swung down, chittering hopefully.

Joe held out a piece of guava, then froze, staring at his hands as if he'd never seen them before. They were normal. All of him was normal.

The monkey chittered angrily, its eyes fixed on the guava.

Joe was stunned. 'How come I'm solid again?'

Fade hastily gave some of her fruit to the monkey. 'The trees did it. They shared their souls with you. They want you to grow strong so you can fight the magician.' She seemed perfectly serious. 'Now we must go and tell Silk you are well again.'

Joe's first day with the bird-children felt like an unexpected holiday. But he soon felt guilty about lazing around when everyone else was so busy. He kept offering to help but everyone just said, 'Rest, Joe Quail! You must be strong enough to fight the magician.'

Eventually, he decided to make the most of it. He'd have to return to the misery of the ruined city soon enough. For now he was contented to spend his time in the dappled beauty of the forest, learning about the life of the bird tribe.

He soon noticed that the younger children were expected to do chores like everyone else. Dressed in miniature gaudy bird-warrior costumes, they followed their elders around, imitating everything they did. They even had their own small knives and spears. At night they nestled together like chicks. Silk explained that after the age of seven or so, bird-children were expected to make tree-homes of their own. After that they slept alone, with only the wind and the wild creatures for company.

No one in Silk's tribe seemed older than thirteen or fourteen. When Joe asked where the children went once they were grown up, everyone looked vague. He got the feeling bird-children preferred to live in the present.

After the day's work was done, the bird-children gathered

around the fire to share their evening meal. And then the music began.

Their songs always began in the same way, Joe noticed, with one singer, or a solo instrument. Then gradually new voices and instruments joined in, building spine-tingling layers of rhythm and harmonies, until it was so beautiful that Joe could hardly bear it.

He caught Silk watching him, her dark eyes sparkling in the firelight.

'I feel as if I've heard these songs before, as if I'm remembering them,' he told her shyly.

She grinned. 'You are in our songs, crazy boy, so of course our songs are in you!'

Equally wonderful were the bird-children's stories describing heroic deeds and magical events, recited enthusiastically from memory, in a mixture of bird and human speech.

Now and then, Joe got the distinct feeling that parts of the narrative were missing. But he couldn't tell if the bird-children had forgotten their lines, or if the story had always been told this way. 'Where do your stories come from?' he asked the skinny boy everyone called Wishbone.

'Our ancestors, of course,' said Wishbone.

Joe's eyes began to grow heavy. He didn't like to ask Silk to give up her tree-home for two nights in a row. But when he asked where he should sleep, she said sternly, 'Our ancestors say you must sleep alone tonight, like a bird-warrior. They say you must dream a true dream.'

Joe thought Silk's ancestors were a bunch of old busybodies, but he knew he couldn't say so.

Silk, Wishbone and sleepy little Fade took a lantern and led Joe through the darkness to the edge of their village. At last they stopped beneath an exceptionally tall tree. Joe stared up at it in dismay.

Silk handed Joe a feathered quilt, then Fade wordlessly showed him a little ladder made of plaited creepers. Under their solemn gaze, Joe climbed up to a dizzy little platform in the branches. By the time he'd reached it, his knees felt like jelly.

Then the bird-children silently melted into the forest, leaving Joe alone in the dark.

He wrapped his quilt around himself, trying to wedge himself securely against the tree trunk. 'Dream a true dream!' he shivered. 'I'll be lucky to sleep a wink!'

But when Joe finally risked looking down from his eyrie, he understood why, out of all the trees in the forest, he had to sleep in this one. From here it was possible to see the unearthly glow of the ruined city where the sorcerer was working his unceasing evil magic.

'Can't tell if it's dusk or dawn,' Joe sang softly. 'Could have been here since I was born.'

The bird-children clearly kept a close watch on the magician's activities. That's why they rescued me, Joe thought. They seemed utterly convinced that he could put things right.

Suddenly he needed to take his mind off the city and its suffering. He raised his head to look at the stars, and caught sight of his favourite Afterdark constellation through the leaves. Spinner had told him it was called the Warrior. It made Joe feel just a little less lonely, seeing its familiar outline glittering in the dark sky.

'If you're listening, ancestors,' he mumbled sleepily, 'I would really appreciate that true dream.'

The rhythmic creaking and swaying of the tree was having a hypnotic effect. Before he knew it, Joe had fallen asleep, bolt upright in his borrowed quilt, as if he'd been sleeping in trees all his life.

He woke as darkness gave way to dawn. For a few minutes he just lay there, listening to the sounds of the forest. Then all at once he remembered his dream.

Joe had been wandering through a shining magical city where he met a child with a wise expression. The child smiled, a calm, sweet smile. Then turning its back on Joe, quite deliberately, it seated itself cross-legged on the ground; and at that moment, Joe woke up.

'Oh well,' he sighed. 'Maybe dreaming true dreams takes practice.' He shinned down his tree, and went to wash his face in a mountain pool.

He had just ducked his head under the water when he heard someone creeping up behind him. Joe jumped up in a panic, spluttering furiously, to face Silk. Her arms seemed to be full of feathers.

'For you. From the ancestors.' She had brought Joe his own warrior costume, decorated with elaborate tribal designs.

'Do I have to wear war-paint too?' he asked nervously.

She nodded. 'You are a bird-warrior now. Sit, I will do it.'

Silk produced some little sticks of vivid colour, and seating herself cross-legged in front of him, she began to paint Joe's face with small careful strokes.

While she worked, Joe told her his disappointing dream.

But Silk obviously had something on her mind. 'Joe Quail,' she said at last. 'You heard many of our stories last night. All of them have wonderful endings. The bad giant is defeated. The brave bird-girl finds the magic phoenix egg. But there is one story which still has no end.'

Joe felt a prickle of excitement. 'What is that story about?'

'It is about you.'

'I'm in one of your *stories*!' No wonder the bird-children had been so thrilled to meet him!

Silk seemed troubled. 'Our story says that things could end in one of two ways. Afterdark will either be plunged into darkness for ever, or –'

'Or light will shine,' Joe whispered.

'The bird-children have dreamed together about this,

and we have decided to mount an attack on the magician and his warriors.'

'I didn't know he had any warriors,' said Joe in dismay.

'Oh yes, thousands and thousands. Anyway, we believe our ancestors wish you to fight with us. We think that's why they sent us to find you.'

'I'm not sure,' said Joe uneasily. And he explained about the magic symbols, which were meant to break the magician's power.

'Without the other two, your symbol is useless,' Silk said firmly. 'It is better you fight with us.'

'I need to think about it,' he told her.

He thought about nothing else all morning.

Silk had great confidence in her mysterious ancestors, but Joe was less sure. The bird-children were wonderfully brave, but he didn't for one moment believe they could defeat the magician in battle. However, an attack might serve to distract the magician, giving Joe one last chance to fulfil the prophecy.

All at once he heard wild war-whoops. 'What's happening?'

'Quill and Spider caught some of the magician's spies!' Fade explained excitedly.

Joe hurried after her. A crowd of bird-children was gathering at the entrance to their village. One of them poked daringly at something with his spear. 'Get off!' it roared.

To his amazement, Joe recognised Kevin's voice.

The younger children backed away. Joe pushed his way to the front, and found his friends trussed up like chickens.

Kevin thrashed around furiously inside the net.

'This isn't helping, you know,' said Flora's voice.

'If you love these bloodthirsty little kids so much, why don't you ask them for their autographs?' he snarled.

Before Joe could speak, Silk dashed up. 'Are you crazy!' she yelled. 'These are Joe's friends!'

Flora peered incredulously through the net. 'Joe! Is that you?'

Kevin shoved her out of the way. His face split into a huge grin. 'Well, it's either that or Big Bird!'

The bird-children hastily untangled Joe's friends. He was so happy to see them he could hardly speak.

'But you're so solid!' cried Flora, hugging him.

'Not to mention feathery,' said Kevin.

All the bird-children whooped and clapped, delighted at the reunion.

Then they fell silent, completely overcome as they recognised the Afterdark princess who featured in the tribe's most exciting stories.

Silk was still mortified by Quill and Spider's mistake.

'Don't be too hard on them,' pleaded Alice. 'They weren't to know.'

'Could have happened to anyone,' Vasco assured them.

That night a feast was held in Alice's honour. This was assembled so swiftly that Joe began to wonder if there was more to the bird-children than he'd suspected. 'Could they be some kind of distant vampire relation?' he asked Flora, as they ate by the light of thousands of little twinkling lights. 'They're very keen on dreams.'

'I suppose,' she said doubtfully.

'They could be tree-vampires,' suggested Kevin mischievously.

As soon as the little ones had gone off to bed, Silk silenced the musicians. It was time for a serious talk.

Neither Alice nor Vasco approved of the bird-children's plan to attack the magician. But Flora and Kevin agreed with Joe. 'It gives us a perfect opportunity to sneak into the city,' said Kevin.

'And do what, exactly?' demanded Vasco. 'We still have no idea what those symbols are for.'

'Maybe we're not meant to,' Flora suggested, 'until we need them, I mean.'

Vasco shook his head. 'That's too risky.'

But eventually Alice and Vasco allowed themselves to be talked round.

'I don't want the bird tribe acting as a distraction, though,' Alice said firmly. 'Too many children have suffered already.'

Wishbone's eyes gleamed in the firelight. 'We may be children, but we are also warriors,' he said.

'Exactly,' said Vasco swiftly. 'Which is why we need you to provide vital back-up.'

Wishbone still looked sullen. 'And what will you do?'

Vasco grinned. 'Alice and I will provide the fun and games.'

Two days later a band of bird-warriors stealthily approached the city. Joe, Kevin and Flora were among them, almost unrecognisable under their war-paint. Alice and Vasco had gone on ahead as agreed.

As they came closer they began to hear sounds of commotion. Suddenly forked lightning split the air.

'Vasco and Alice are stirring things up nicely,' Kevin hissed.

Joe met Silk's eyes. 'This is it,' he whispered. 'This is where we find out how your story ends.'

'The end is not your business, crazy boy,' she whispered back. 'Your business is to be strong and —'

'I know, I know,' he grinned. 'And fight the magician!'

More lightning zigzagged dramatically overhead.

Whispering hasty goodbyes to Silk and her people, the children darted into the ruins to find a scene of total chaos.

A bunch of agitated ghouls rushed about, trying to dodge the biggest thunderbolts Joe had ever seen.

There was another flash, and Joe caught a dazzling glimpse of Vasco and Alice, high in the turret of a ruined tower. From this distance they looked like tiny figures in a doll's house.

A sizzling pink thunderbolt zoomed down to earth.

Kevin chuckled. 'Bet that's Vasco.'

Under cover of this daring display of sorcery, Joe led Flora and Kevin to the pyramid where he had been a slave.

Suddenly Kevin went rigid.

'What is it?' Joe followed his friend's horrified gaze. A knot of cloud was forming in the sky. The cloud became a thin shadowy hand.

'No!' whispered Flora.

The hand expanded until it blotted out the sun. Then, stretching out thin, spidery fingers, it began to grope blindly towards the tower.

The tiny figures rushed pathetically from one side of the tower to the other, trying to stay out of reach. But it was no use.

They watched, paralysed, as the hand wrapped itself around Alice and Vasco like a fist, until there was nothing left but shadow.

Then the hand faded as suddenly as it came.

And Alice and Vasco had gone.

13
The lost city

The children clung together for comfort.

'Will he kill them?' Flora wept.

Kevin shook his head. 'Killing's too simple,' he said grimly. 'He's the type who likes to put on a show, know what I mean?'

Something inside Joe seemed to have turned to stone. Without Alice, there was no point in carrying on. Then in a rough voice he hardly recognised, he heard himself say, 'We've got to stick to the plan. That's what they'd want us to do.'

He didn't say that without Alice and Vasco, there was no way of getting back to their own world. He'd always known it could end like this. He just hadn't wanted to believe it.

Flora seemed utterly dazed. 'It's over,' she whispered. 'We're done for.'

'Let's get moving,' Joe barked. 'The ghouls will be back any minute!'

As he bullied them to carry on, he felt as if he was watching himself from some cold, distant place. Was this an older, wiser Joe who saw patterns in the stars? If so, Joe hated him.

But it worked.

Flora pulled herself together. 'You're right. We've got to do this for Clare and the others.'

Kevin dashed his hand across his eyes. 'Yeah. It's not over till it's over, right?'

The children ran towards the entrance, painstakingly unblocked by the magician's slaves. Now the rubble had been cleared away, the doorway looked unpleasantly like a huge gaping mouth.

'At least it hasn't got teeth,' said Flora bravely.

'Not that we can see,' muttered Kevin.

But on the other side of the entrance, they shielded their eyes, amazed. The pyramid was filled with sunshine.

The light had no obvious source, yet everything shone as bright as day. It was like the magic chamber, Joe thought, only a hundred times brighter.

Kevin looked stunned. 'You do realise this place is covered in gold?'

What kind of gold shines like the sun, Joe wondered to himself?

As their eyes adjusted, the children saw that they were at the top of a flight of stairs. Below them was a golden passageway. It appeared to go under the pyramid. 'Looks like it's this way!' said Joe.

Kevin looked uneasy. 'Anything could be down there.'

'Something *is* down there,' said Joe. 'Why do you think the magician made us shift those rocks?'

Kevin didn't move.

'We've got to check it out, Kevin,' Joe insisted. 'It's our only hope.'

'So everyone keeps saying. But if you ask me, our hope just ran out a few minutes ago.'

To the boys' amazement, Flora stood on tiptoe and kissed Kevin on the cheek. 'Come on, Kev. Like you said. It's not over till it's over.'

Kevin gave her a tired smile. 'You feisty vampire girl, you.'

'You'd better believe it,' she told him.

They hurried down the stairs and into the passage.

After a few metres the passage sloped steeply downwards, twisting and turning as it went. The golden floor was as smooth as glass. Once or twice, Joe almost lost his footing.

They were being lead deep into the earth, yet the air was surprisingly fresh and sweet.

Suddenly Flora looked dismayed. 'Uh-oh. There's a door.'

'And what a door!' breathed Kevin.

Like the rest of the pyramid, the door was constructed on a massive scale. Unfortunately there was no handle and no visible lock of any kind.

Flora rushed up to it hopefully, but the door remained closed. She stamped her foot. 'Why won't it let us in!'

'This isn't Sainsbury's, Flo,' said Kevin mildly.

Joe studied the door closely. It was divided into hundreds of tiny, highly-decorated squares. Each square contained a symbol. His heart missed a beat. He could see his symbol! The magic eye.

He turned excitedly to Flora. But she had seen for herself. '*That's* what the symbols were for!' she crowed. 'You find your symbol, then you push it in, like a keypad.'

'Is yours here?' he asked.

She nodded confidently. 'It's the flame.'

'Mine's that wavy one,' said Kevin. Joe knocked his hand away. 'Don't!' he said. 'Not until you're one hundred percent positive. You don't know what will happen if we hit the wrong ones.'

Kevin pulled a face. 'Like we know what'll happen if we hit the right ones!'

'Let's do it on three, before anyone can wimp out,' suggested Flora. 'One, two –'

But before Flora got to three, they heard a deadly sigh, as if all the air was being sucked out of the pyramid.

'He's coming after us! Quick! Press the symbols!' Joe yelled. 'We can still do it, we can!'

But at the last minute, Flora pulled back her hand. 'It's not mine! I thought it was, but it's the wrong colour!' She scanned the symbols frantically. 'Joe, I can't see it!'

'Look harder! It's there!'

'Hurry up,' moaned Kevin.

Flora lunged wildly at a tiny flame pattern.

'We've got to do it together, dummy!' Joe roared. 'One, two, three!'

All three children simultaneously hit their symbols.

The groans and rumbling sounds seemed to come from the earth itself. Slowly and agonisingly, the door began to open. It didn't sound like a door. It sounded like a forest uprooting itself, tree by painful tree.

'Come *on!*' Kevin screamed.

We're not going to make it, Joe thought in despair.

Then he felt an icy whisper on the back of his neck.

Joe couldn't help himself; he glanced wildly over his shoulder and saw a shapeless creature billowing towards him like fog.

He froze, paralysed with terror.

'NO!' screamed his sister, breaking the spell. And with Flora yanking Joe furiously on one side, and Kevin barging against him on the other, the three children scraped through the tiny opening, and slammed the door shut, trapping the terrifying creature outside.

They held on to each other briefly. Then Joe stared around him wonderingly. 'This was in my dream!'

Kevin looked as if he didn't know whether to laugh or cry. 'It's beautiful!'

'It's magic,' Flora whispered.

Butterflies, like scraps of coloured silk, fluttered softly from flower to flower. The sweet-scented air was filled with birdsong and the calm splashing of fountains.

Joe couldn't believe it. They had found the magic city. There was no need for enchantments to restore it. It was already perfect.

In delicate shades of rose and gold and sandalwood, the lost city glowed like an underground sunrise.

The children set off through the lovely silent streets.

'No one's lived here for centuries,' said Joe. 'Why isn't it overgrown and cobwebby?'

'Like some spooky museum,' Flora agreed. 'But it feels so *alive!*'

They stopped beside a pool where tiny iris and water-lilies grew. The water danced and sparkled with a glistening light of its own.

Joe gazed at their joined reflections, and with a rush of wonder, recognised the picture in the prophecy. They had become the children in the book at last!

'I can't get my head round this,' muttered Kevin. 'All those poor slaves grubbing in the dust, doing that nutter's lost city jigsaw puzzle, and the true city was down here all the time.'

They had reached a tree-lined avenue, wide enough to allow them to walk side by side. Overhead, graceful palms clicked their fronds in the breeze.

And there ahead of them was a shining temple.

Its curving roof gave it the appearance of some wonderful winged creature. The building seemed to float, like a creation of air.

'If you had a key to your nice little magic city, and you wanted to keep it safe, where would you put it?' asked Kevin.

They stared at him. Then without a word, all three children began to run towards the temple.

But when they reached the foot of the steps, they saw that their way was barred by two imposing golden statues. They were identical to the stone cats Joe had seen in the ruined city, except for having their snooty expressions intact.

'I can't stand it! We're so close!' Flora brightened. 'Maybe we should try our symbols again.'

'Maybe,' agreed Joe doubtfully.

They started up the steps. Suddenly they heard a sharp exhalation, like someone letting air out of a tyre. The statues were hissing!

'They're alive!' squeaked Flora.

Before the children could turn and run, the cats spoke in unison.

'Three heroes set out,' they chanted, 'but only one is chosen.'

Joe felt the tiny hairs stand up on the back of his neck.

'Beg pardon?' said Kevin.

'Ssh, it's a riddle,' said Flora. 'We've got to answer it, then they'll let us in.'

There was an edgy pause.

'Maybe we could just hear that hero thing again?' suggested Kevin.

The cats ignored him. 'Step forward, O chosen child!' they yowled. Their singsong voices sounded distinctly unfriendly.

'Sorry, we don't know anything about any chosen child,' Flora said politely. 'It didn't say about one in the prophecy.'

'Chosen child, accept your fate!' warbled the golden cats, as if she hadn't spoken. 'Climb the steps. Unlock the gate!'

Kevin lost his temper. 'I've had enough of this! Mysterious prophecies, weird symbols and chosen children! Doesn't anyone do anything *normally* round here?' He went storming up the steps.

What's he going to do, thought Joe nervously? Head-butt them?

The cats gave a low sulphurous hiss.

'Don't, Kevin! They'll hurt you!' cried Flora. 'They're the temple guardians. They can't just let anyone in!'

'Let them explain, Kev,' Joe pleaded.

Kevin stopped in mid-stride. 'All right. But it had better not be in poetry.' He glared at the cats. 'You were saying?'

There was a tense silence. Joe was terrified Kevin had

offended them. But the beasts had apparently taken his criticism to heart, because all at once they spoke again, but without a trace of poetry.

'For security purposes, the temple gates are not visible to the general public, OK?' they gabbled. 'These gates will appear, if, and only if, the chosen child – in other words, the right kid – passes between the temple guardians. In other words, US!' they hissed.

'And if it's the wrong kid?' asked Kevin suspiciously.

'Our breath will destroy you,' intoned the cats.

'What, you'll like, slay us with your stinky pussy-cat breath!' he jeered.

'Actually, we use fire!' said the cats hollowly.

Kevin's expression changed to one of extreme alarm. He dived hastily out of range, as the beasts blew out twin blasts of scorching flame.

Kevin ran his hands over his stubble. 'That had better all be there,' he muttered. He retreated down the steps and pulled Joe and Flora into a huddle. 'Here's what we do,' he hissed. 'They've got their hearts set on this chosen child, so I say we flip a coin. Whoever gets best of three, gets to try their luck.'

Flora swallowed. 'I can't see another way,' she agreed bravely. 'And one in three is *fairly* good odds.'

But Joe felt sure that picking a chosen child wasn't a question of luck. For once he didn't have to think. This was *his* task. It was why the bird-children's ancestors had sent him that oddly confusing dream. It no longer bothered Joe that his dream still made absolutely no sense to him. He had the feeling that magic was like advanced maths. A vampire genius like Flora could probably figure out what it meant. Joe just knew without a shadow of doubt that his dream message was true. Without a word to his friends, he went bounding up the steps.

'Come back, you madman! Do you want to get fried?' yelled Kevin.

'I know what I'm doing, OK,' Joe called.

By the time he reached the top of the steps, he was less confident. Close up, the temple guardians looked alarmingly ominous.

Don't think, Joe told himself. Just do it.

He made to slip between the giant beasts. Their unsmiling lips drew back. Fiery breath grazed his cheek. He smelled a sweet spicy perfume, like strong incense. Flora cried out a warning.

But before Joe could panic, there was a chime of magic and a dark archway appeared. The guardians had just been giving Joe their blessing.

They yowled out their congratulations. 'But take care!' they sighed behind him. 'Now the chosen child has opened the path, others may follow.'

'What others?' Joe heard Flora call anxiously.

But he didn't really take it in. He was still dizzy with relief.

Flora and Kevin came galloping up behind him.

'We're sticking with you, mate. What with you being the *chosen* child and everything,' Kevin grinned.

Beyond the archway, Joe could see only darkness. His heart sank. 'Better stick with Flora,' he sighed. 'She can see in the dark.' Was it his imagination, or had they spent this entire adventure moving from light to shadow and back again?

But the instant the children passed beneath the arch, torches blazed up on either side. As they walked on, new torches sprang into life, guiding them deeper into the belly of the temple.

After a while, there was no need for torches. The air was growing brighter, though Joe could see no obvious source of light. Then they turned a corner, and everyone gasped.

It was like walking into a huge, living diamond. Every surface shimmered and shone.

Joe stared upwards in awe. Sunlight flooded down from a skylight so high that from where they stood it seemed no bigger than a pinhead. It was this tiny pin-prick of light, reflecting off cleverly-placed prisms and crystals, which gave the temple its extraordinary radiance.

This light wasn't simply something to see by. It was alive.

Joe turned his face into the dazzling downpour.

Everything's going to be all right, he thought. I can feel it.

Flora stretched out her arms happily, twizzling like a dancer. 'I could stay here for ever, couldn't you?'

'Yeah, you just know nothing bad could happen here,' Joe agreed.

Then he saw Flora's expression change.

'What is it?' he asked anxiously.

His sister seemed to have lost the power of speech.

Joe forced himself to turn around.

Behind him stood a host of grinning ghouls. Hovering over their heads was a cloudy swirling form.

Joe had unlocked the lost city for the magician.

14

In the crystal chamber

Their enemy floated down to earth and took on the shape of a human being.

He seemed to be aiming for a child's picture-book version of a magician; wild flowing locks, a cloak richly spattered with moons and stars, and a broad-brimmed magician's hat.

'I don't know why you're so shocked! Any Tom, Dick or Harry can waltz in, once the chosen child has opened the way. Seems like those magic kids weren't as smart as everyone thought,' the sorcerer added spitefully.

Suddenly, without appearing to move, he was peering right into their faces as if they were animals in a zoo. His expression became curiously soft and open. He reached out his hand, apparently enchanted by these beings from another world.

All three children backed away hastily.

A flicker of disappointment crossed the sorcerer's face, but in a flash it had gone, and like some playful big brother he was all smiles. 'Manners!' he teased. 'Oh, all right, *I'll* do the introductions, shall I? After all, I feel as if I know you quite well by this time. Let's see. You're Kevin. You must be Joe, and this is the little vampire girl. And I'm –'

The magician broke off, looking self-conscious. 'To be honest, this name thing is a real headache. I still can't come up with one that really suits my personality. Maybe you can help?'

Kevin muttered something unprintable.

Joe couldn't understand why the magician filled him with such horror. He wasn't particularly tall or frightening-looking. His face was really extraordinarily sweet, with a child's bright wondering eyes.

In fact, contained in its Disney World cloak, the magician's cloudy shape seemed quite appealing. Like someone you could maybe win round.

Then Joe looked closer and shuddered with revulsion.

Under the surface of the magician's skin, sinister colours flickered and sparkled. Doing battle with this unstable creature would be like fighting a ball of poisonous gas.

The magician suddenly went into fits of laughter. 'It's tragic!' he crowed. 'Three children setting out to conquer the most powerful sorcerer there has ever been, or ever will be.'

Kevin's face twisted. 'Don't think much of yourself, do you?'

'Kevin, don't,' pleaded Flora.

'I was hoping you'd be fun,' the magician continued

scornfully. 'But it was just too easy to be a real challenge. Like taking candy from a baby.'

'We'll take your word for that,' muttered Kevin.

'Stop it!' Flora begged. 'You'll make him really mad.'

'Oh, like he's totally well-adjusted now,' Kevin growled.

'And you were SO predictable! I had you in my sights night and day.'

'Liar,' said Joe, stung. 'Not the *whole* time, you didn't.'

'Oh, I think I did, Joe!' the magician sang out triumphantly. 'I monitored your movements from the moment you left that sad little museum, until you turned up on my doorstep. Did you think I came across you in the desert by *accident?*' His skin flashed and flickered like the northern lights.

'Sorry, mate, but I think we might have noticed you in the desert,' objected Kevin. 'Unless you were disguised as one of them big bald birdies.'

The magician thrust his face menacingly into Kevin's. 'Guess again,' he snarled. Then he danced away, laughing, this terrifying child who had never grown up.

'Oh, all right,' he sighed. 'I suppose I'd better give you a clue, otherwise we'll be here all day!'

In a husky little voice he sang, 'If you loved me in sequins, you'll adore me in blue!' And the magician's skin shimmered through a dazzling spectrum of blues, from lavender to indigo.

Joe's heart gave a lurch of horror. 'It was you,' he whispered. 'You were the mirage magic show.'

Flora looked as if she might be sick.

'You seem upset, Flora. Ask her why she's so upset, Joe. Ooh, Joe's going to *love* this,' the magician gloated.

Joe clenched his fists. 'Leave my sister alone!'

'Don't!' Flora's face was pinched with distress. 'He's right, Joe. It's all my fault.'

He was bewildered. 'What are you talking about?'

Flora slid her hand into her top and miserably pulled out a strange, dark jewel. With a pang of dismay he recognised the storm-stone.

The magician had a peculiarly hungry expression. 'A stone in her shoe!' he quoted admiringly. 'Your sister's a born liar. A natural!'

Joe felt numb. He had trusted Flora absolutely. Suddenly nothing in his life felt real.

Tears spilled down Flora's cheeks. 'I took it because I wanted to tell Clare – I mean, I needed –' She struggled for words. 'Because I – I miss my mum so much,' she blurted out at last.

Joe still didn't trust himself to speak.

'He knew I'd take it. He's been using it like a tracking device. He got to you through me, Joe.'

The magician was almost hugging himself with glee. 'What she's trying to say is that she betrayed you, purely so she could impress Clare. Unbelievable, isn't it? Thanks to your sister, Joe, I've got you all completely in my power.'

Flora seemed dangerously near collapse, yet somehow she went on standing there, white and swaying, defying Joe to hate her.

He longed to comfort her, but the magician's gloating words swirled around in his head like smoke, and he couldn't think straight.

'I'm so sorry, Joe,' she choked. 'If it makes you feel any better, I wish I'd never been born!'

And suddenly she ripped the storm-stone off its chain. It sailed through the air, landing close to Joe's foot.

Kevin cleared his throat. 'You don't have to say sorry to me, Flo. That *thing* over there set you up.'

Joe finally found his voice. 'It wasn't you who let these sickos in here, Flora. The chosen child,' he added bitterly. 'That's a joke.'

The magician made a flamboyant gesture. 'Time for a newsflash!'

To the children's dismay, Vasco and Alice's faces appeared, reflected again and again in the chamber's many prisms. They had been imprisoned in a repulsive kind of cocoon. They were deathly pale; their eyes empty.

'You destroy everything good,' Joe said shakily. 'That's what you do.'

'Of course,' the magician agreed. 'Why change the world,

when it's SO much more fun to destroy it!'

Suddenly Joe was filled with grim determination. Their quest mustn't end like this. They couldn't defeat this monstrous creature. But just because they couldn't win, it didn't mean they couldn't put up a fight.

Hidden under his feathered tunic was Wishbone's parting gift, a pouch containing a small but deadly knife. But it wasn't the knife Joe wanted. He slid his hand stealthily into the pouch, and closed his fingers around Spinner's slingshot.

Joe would only get one chance at this. He edged invisibly closer to the storm-stone, until he felt it touching his foot, his heart beating wildly.

Sensing Joe was up to something, Kevin gave the tiniest of nods.

'I've enjoyed our chat,' the magician was saying. 'But we really must get down to business. It's a pain, but I need you to find that key. The one that will finally make me master of this delightful little city.'

Joe silently asked the children who had built this lovely temple to forgive him for what he was about to do.

The magician's mood changed abruptly. His skin glittered with menace. 'To be honest, I'm getting irritated now. And when I'm irritated, I become *dangerously* unpredictable —'

Joe snatched up the storm-stone and fired it wildly into the air.

It flew like a bird, soaring up and up, until Joe began to

think it would never stop. Then all the crystals dimmed at once. And before either the magician or his ghouls could react, the chamber exploded into a glittering galaxy of fragments.

'Run!' screamed Joe. He and Kevin grabbed Flora's hands. They pulled her through the shining crystal rain, and out into the main part of the temple.

'Not the front way,' gasped Flora. 'There'll be ghouls. There's a side-door, I noticed it on the way in.'

But the door was closed.

'I'm sorry, I'm sorry,' Flora moaned. 'He's going to catch us and it'll be my fault. I ruin everything.'

Joe put his arm round her. 'It's all right, Flo,' he said shakily. 'I just wanted to give that creepy lizard a run for his money.'

Then just as everything seemed hopeless, they saw a starry light coming towards them.

'It can't be,' whispered Kevin.

'It is!' shrieked Flora.

Suddenly they were all running madly towards the light. And unbelievably there was Alice, apparently untouched by her ordeal. 'Thank goodness you're safe! Vasco and I escaped as soon as we could.'

'Oh, this is so wonderful. We thought you were dead.' Flora reached out to touch her, but the princess stepped lightly sideways and Flora's hand closed on empty air.

'We have little time. Vasco's got the magician cornered in the crystal chamber, but he won't be able to hold him for long. We *have* to find that key!' Alice began to hurry them towards the temple entrance.

'But we don't know where to look,' panted Joe. 'We thought it was in the temple, only it wasn't.'

'Then it must be hidden in one of the other buildings. Come on, think,' Alice ordered, marching them past the temple guardians, who stayed disappointingly silent.

Kevin sounded desperate. 'But we can't search the whole city.'

'Why not?' she demanded.

Joe shook his head. 'This is all wrong. We're assuming this key is something incredibly complicated. Something secret and hidden.'

Flora stared at him. 'Joe, you're right! That's what grown-ups do, locking up their valuables. Using weird codes and PIN numbers.'

'But the kids who made this city weren't like that,' Joe explained. 'They were more like the bird-tribe kids. This city belonged to all of them. If you ask me, the magic was just *there*, like – like electricity, or water. That way, any child who wanted could use it.'

Alice sighed. 'This is all very interesting, but I really haven't got time to listen to long speeches, Joe. Are you saying this key is actually something ridiculously obvious?'

Joe tried not to feel hurt. 'Kind of.' Alice had never spoken to him so sharply before. It made him feel a bit funny around the knees.

They had reached the avenue of palm trees. Joe felt a twinge of alarm. He couldn't see a single bird or butterfly anywhere.

Kevin glanced around edgily. 'Help us out, Flo,' he pleaded. 'You're the girl genius. The Wizard of Oz is going to come scorching down those steps any moment, and we'll be back to square one.'

'Honestly, Kevin,' Flora snapped. 'You're such a loser.'

Kevin flushed. 'That's nice. Coming from a sneaky little thief.'

'Now, now, children.' Alice sounded almost amused.

They were passing the pool they had seen on their way to the temple.

Joe gazed wistfully at the sparkling water, remembering how astonished he had felt at their transformed reflections.

He had the nagging feeling that something was wrong. But he was just being stupid. Not only were Alice and Vasco safe after all, but they were on the verge of finding the vital key. So why wasn't everyone more excited? Why were they all so tired and bad-tempered?

Flora was smiling her crooked little smile. 'I'd rather be a thief than a yobbo like you, Kevin Kitchener,' she said sweetly.

Joe heard himself snap, 'At least he's human!'

Flora burst into peals of mirth. 'Help! Help! The chosen child has cut me to the quick!'

Joe ran at Flora in a fury, and barged her over the edge of the pool. They were standing beside the shallow end, so Flora wasn't in serious danger. But he was instantly horrified at what he'd done.

His sister clambered back out, dripping wet. 'I'll get you for that, Joe Quail!' She stamped her boot with rage.

There was an ominous cracking sound.

Everyone jumped out of the way as the pavement Flora had been standing on shattered into pieces.

'Flaming Norah!' said Kevin, shaken.

'I didn't stamp that hard,' Flora wailed.

'Now that *is* interesting,' mused Alice.

Flora warily inspected the results of her temper tantrum. She gave a nervous giggle. 'Ooh-er,' she said. 'I'm not showing off or anything, but I think I just acquired magic powers!'

The children exchanged awed glances. Then they fell about laughing.

'You said it, Joe,' Kevin sang out. 'Like electricity, or *water*, you said!'

'We're so dense!' Joe cried. 'We never thought about pools!'

Flora flung her arms round his neck. 'Who cares, we got there in the end. The prophecy was right!'

'Nice one, Joe!' chortled Kevin. 'You just pushed your sister into the city's sacred power source.'

They turned to Alice excitedly. But Alice wasn't there.

In her place was a triumphant figure in a star-splattered cloak.

'Out of my way,' he snarled. 'This is a very special moment, and I don't want it spoiled by a bunch of interfering little brats.'

Flora backed away. 'No! It can't have been you.'

'You total scum!' yelled Kevin.

'You smelled funny,' said Joe stupidly. 'I knew there was something. You just didn't *smell* like Alice.'

'Now where would you say was the deepest part?' the sorcerer pondered aloud. 'Ah yes!' He gave the children a cheery wave. 'Back in five! Oh, while I'm gone, see if you can come up with a name. Something — I don't know — *incandescent*. Of course, I'll be unbearably magnificent by then!'

And with a swirl of his starry cloak, the magician dived into the pool, and instantly vanished from sight.

Joe stood paralysed with horror, trying not to think about the creature wallowing below them in the pure water of the lake.

They had made a final, fatal mistake.

Now everything they loved was going to be destroyed.

15
The end of the game

Nothing disturbed the magical stillness of the pool.

'Shouldn't there be bubbles?' Kevin muttered. 'Even titchy little frogs make bubbles.'

'He's been down there ages.' There was a tinge of excitement in Flora's voice.

The children exchanged wary glances. Was it possible the indestructible magician had drowned?

Kevin's face clouded. 'Ugh!'

A sinister film floated to the top of the pool. It oozed across the surface, thickening as it spread. A deadly chill crept into the air. The waterlilies drooped their heads.

They had time to run, but somehow the children no longer had the heart to save themselves. They huddled together like orphans.

The slime began to bubble like a stew. With hideous squelching sounds, an unseen force sucked every trace of sludge into the centre of the pool. A monstrous figure began to form.

'He's bigger, all right. But you can't honestly say he's improved,' said Kevin shakily.

They watched helplessly, as their enemy slowly rematerialised from the sludge.

Something inside Joe seemed to break. We can't run. We can't fight, he thought numbly. We may as well just lie down and die. Then the words of the prophecy floated back to him.

By winning they will lose. By losing they will win.

Flora gave him a startled look. Without meaning to, Joe had spoken aloud. 'Say that again,' she said.

Joe shuddered as the figure shook off its coat of slime.

'I said say it *again!*' Flora shrieked. 'It's *important.*'

The sorcerer was every bit as magnificent as he had promised. He looked as if he had been cut out of the night sky. Beneath his skin, glorious new constellations glittered and whirled.

Flora planted herself furiously between Joe and the magician, and screamed into his face. 'I want to know what you just said!'

'OK, OK,' Joe said hurriedly. 'By winning they will lose. By losing they will win.'

Kevin clenched his teeth. 'I'm going to die! I can do without the poetry.'

In a trance, Joe saw the waters part, allowing the sorcerer to pass.

Flora was eerily calm. 'Joe, listen! I've got it! It's like what I was saying about bullies. Fighting is useless. And running away makes them more powerful. The only thing you can do is switch off and let them win!'

Joe tried to take in what his sister was telling him.

The magician was climbing back on to dry land. As his starry boots made contact with the earth, Joe heard a prolonged and dreadful hiss. 'You mean, just give up?' he said wildly.

She shook her head. 'I mean – let go.'

Kevin's expression changed. 'Stop playing his game, you mean?'

'Quickly hold hands,' she cried. 'No, wait! Sit down, then hold hands!'

Shaking all over, Joe sat down with his back to the magician. This is the saddest, most totally doomed thing I have done in my life, he told himself miserably.

Now they had linked hands, the children formed a wobbly human triangle. The magician began to laugh triumphantly, a nightmare sound which seemed to come from everywhere and nowhere.

'Don't think about him,' said Flora fiercely. 'Don't even *care* about him. Just let this whole magician business go, OK?'

All around them, the city was losing its lovely glow.

This is how it would be, for ever and ever, Joe thought.

Once the magician had drained all the goodness and beauty from the magic city, it would be the turn of Afterdark, and after that Joe's own world. And Joe was supposed to sit here like a dummy and take it?

They had begun to lean inwards, until their heads were touching, unconsciously turning their doomed human triangle into an equally doomed pyramid.

I wonder why we did that, Joe thought.

And suddenly he felt the butterfly touch of magical minds against his own. 'In winning we lose,' he whispered. 'In losing we win.'

A wind scudded across the lily-pond, catching up the dead flower petals and whirling them away.

'You know why this city is fading, don't you?' the sorcerer yelled exultantly. 'It's because all this glorious magic is going into ME!'

If Joe shut his eyes, he could see the Afterdark princess. Not as he had last seen her, lifeless in that evil cocoon, nor the fake Alice with her cold smile, but her true self, her grey eyes alive with laughter.

You were my best thing, he told her silently. I mean, I'm glad I saw this city, and met the bird-children and slept in a tree, but you were my best best thing.

'You're missing a once-in-a-lifetime experience here,' the magician sang out. 'This is my moment of triumph! Don't you even want to WATCH?'

If Joe had to die, let it be like this, he thought, feeling their shared strength flowing back and forth. He didn't glance round to see when the magician was going to pounce. He didn't check how huge and terrifying their enemy had grown. He just kept his attention on the wonderful life-giving current flowing between their joined hands, feeling perfectly at peace.

Without knowing he was going to, Joe spoke aloud to the magician. 'It's all right,' he said quietly. 'You win.' Then he went back to concentrating on his hands.

Flora gasped. 'Joe, look!'

He smiled dreamily. Whatever happens, we're free, he thought.

Kevin's voice was urgent. 'Seriously, you've got to check this out.'

Joe was only just in time.

The tiny swirling galaxies trapped under the magician's skin had grown dangerously bright. It hurt Joe's eyes to look at them. With a thrill of horror, he saw how it would end.

Of the magician's true self, only a few shadowy threads remained. His massive overdose of stolen magic was causing them to snap, one by one.

The magician seemed unaware of what was happening. He gazed down at himself, completely overcome. 'I am a god!' he gasped.

'There's just one problem, mate,' said Kevin softly. 'You're not real.'

Glowing cracks appeared all over the magician's body. For one breathtaking instant, he lit up from head to foot.

There was a sudden electric hush, before the magician blew apart into billions of multi-coloured particles. The fragments rained softly from the sky, bright and harmless as confetti.

Then a dark bird-like shape fluttered down.

The children nervously backed away from the star-splattered garment billowing on the ground. It seemed to be burning, yet there were no visible flames. They watched, holding their breath. But it continued to shrivel steadily until there was nothing left of the magician's cloak but a heap of glittering ash.

And then they knew for sure that it was over.

The children exchanged stunned smiles.

'We did it,' breathed Joe. 'We actually did it!' Suddenly, he felt strangely dizzy.

'Joe!' said Flora sharply. 'What's happening?'

He glanced down anxiously, then a great wave of relief washed over him as he saw that his dream body was starting to fade. He was going home.

16
The midnight museum

'I hope Joe's OK,' said Flora anxiously. 'That was a real smile, right? He wasn't just being brave?'

Kevin grinned. 'He'll be fine. When bad magicians go up in smoke, their wicked works go with them, remember?'

'All the same. It's spooky, seeing your brother melt. Plus he's missing this!'

They watched in silence as the colours flooded back into the lost city.

Flora gazed wonderingly into the pool, which was clear and sparkling again. 'You're right, Kevin,' she said softly. 'You'd never know he'd been here. It's all gone, every trace of dark magic. Even the lilies have grown back.'

Kevin gave a sigh of relief. 'Which means that sick cocoon-thing has gone too.' He grabbed her hand. 'Come on! Alice will be worrying.'

Flora gave the city a last yearning look. 'We'll never see this again, will we?'

Kevin shook his head. 'Probably not.'

Night was falling as they emerged from the ruined pyramid. Flora sniffed the air. 'I hated the way the magician never let it get dark, didn't you? No vampire would *ever* do that.'

'Listen,' said Kevin. 'What can you hear?'

She frowned. 'Nothing.'

'Exactly! No cries, no jangling chains, no horrible wind blowing heaps of dust about. Just total peace and quiet.'

All at once Flora did hear something; faint sounds of music and drumming. A bright flicker of torches came bobbing through the dusk.

The bird tribe had come to welcome them back in style.

As they approached, Silk's face fell. She'd been hoping to see Joe, Flora thought. But the bird-girl quickly recovered herself. 'Did that crazy boy get home safely?' she demanded.

'I hope so,' sighed Flora.

'Yes,' said Kevin firmly.

Silk fiddled with her bangles. 'Did he fight with great courage?' she asked casually.

The bird-children gathered round in silence as Flora described all that had happened. She did her best to make the scary bits as thrilling as possible, but their painted faces showed absolutely no sign of emotion,

'I'll tell you what was weird,' she said desperately. 'There was this moment, when everything seemed completely lost. But we went on, holding hands in our silly little human pyramid, and suddenly the city went completely still. And I

just bickering light-heartedly as they toiled to the top of the sand dunes.

All at once familiar starry rays shone through the dark.

Flora's heart gave a leap of happiness. She heard Vasco say excitedly, 'You know, when I woke up in that disgusting cocoon, I had this great idea. And I think you're going to love it.'

Then Kevin took Flora's hand. 'Come on, bat-girl. Time to go home.'

It was Saturday morning and Joe was in a terrible mood.

'You should have stayed at home if you're going to be such a party pooper, Joe,' Flora complained.

But as they headed towards the old part of town, Joe's trainers felt as if they were filled with lead.

'You can't exactly call it a party,' he objected.

'Sure it is,' grinned Kevin. 'A working party.'

'It's perfect,' said Flora earnestly. 'I don't know why you can't see how perfect it is. Plus Vasco really needs a job, now Dream Catchers has closed down.'

'You've got to admit, he'll be brilliant,' said Kevin.

'I said I'd help, didn't I?' growled Joe.

They turned down the run-down street which led to the river.

'I just said I liked the museum the way it was,' he grumbled. 'That's all.'

What he'd really loved was that it had been a secret, just between them and Alice. But to say so would make Joe look like some spoiled kid.

He trailed after them down the alleyway. Kevin and Flora waited for him to catch up.

'Looks great, doesn't it?' said Flora in a hopeful voice.

If they were waiting for him to ooh and aah, they could wait for ever, Joe thought. He stuck his hands in his pockets, glowering.

Kevin sounded hurt. 'Vasco's been working like a dog.'

'Don't you love the new sign?' Flora read it aloud, as though Joe couldn't do it for himself. 'The Midnight Museum,' she breathed happily. 'Just think, it's a little piece of Afterdark, right here in our town.'

The star-splattered sign reminded Joe of the magician, seconds before he blew apart. But he didn't say that either.

'It's OK,' he said grudgingly.

'It's still a mess inside,' said Kevin as they walked around to the back of the building. 'And they haven't got the café up and running yet.'

In the courtyard, Clare Ying's brother was sanding down an old table. 'Go in. The door's open.'

Vasco's voice wafted from an upstairs window. 'Of course, it will be so much more than an after-school club . . .' he was explaining smoothly to someone.

Joe went inside. To his surprise, the ground floor seemed

absolutely huge. Clare was busily unpacking the few boxes which remained. 'Hi!' she beamed. 'I just found loads of amazing Afterdark games.'

Joe heard Flora say excitedly, 'Oh, I love this one. Joe and I played it all the time when we were on the ranger ship.'

'Did Spinner ever find his little girls, do you know?' Clare asked.

Flora sighed. 'That's what's so sad. I mean, if anyone deserves a happy ending . . .'

Joe didn't want to hear any more. Instead he went looking for Alice. He found her on the next floor, carefully tipping paint into a shallow tray.

He lifted a corner of one of the dustsheets, and dropped it hastily. 'You've still got that creepy harp, then,' he said in a sour voice.

She grinned. 'Wait till you see what Clare found in some of those boxes!'

Suddenly all Joe's mixed feelings boiled over. 'I don't understand,' he blurted out. 'All these kids who come to your after-school club or whatever. What will they think about stuff like nightingale harps and books of magic riddles?'

Alice dipped her roller in the paint. 'If they're not ready, they won't notice.'

He stared at her. 'Honestly?'

'Honestly. They'll just have a great time and go home and play computer games.'

'What about the other kids?' he said warily. 'The ones who are ready.'

Alice's grey eyes held a glint of mischief. 'Well, I suppose they'll be starting out on a never-ending adventure. Like you, Joe.'

She began to cover the dingy wall with glowing colour.

Joe felt a rush of happiness so violent he had to turn away. She means it isn't over, he thought exultantly. The magic will never, ever be over.

And suddenly he couldn't remember what he'd been worried about.

He shared Alice with Flora and Kevin, didn't he? And that worked out all right. They were a team. As individuals they were quite special obviously. But together they definitely had what it took.

And now there was Clare. Lately she and Flora spent hours on the phone. After one of their talks, Flora practically floated into Joe's room. 'Clare says I'm the deepest person she knows,' she told him incredulously. 'She thinks it's to do with me being a vampire.'

Joe watched dreamily as Alice loaded her brush with more paint.

'Can people ever be happy in both worlds?' he asked suddenly.

'I am, Joe,' said Alice calmly. 'How about you?'

He helped himself to a roller and set to work beside the open window.

Down in the courtyard, Flora was talking to a little boy and his elder brother. Joe had the feeling he'd seen them before. Then it clicked.

They were with Clare in the tunnel, he remembered. They helped us escape.

Just then Flora came marching up the stairs, wearing her most determined expression.

Behind her was Colin, his eyes huge with awe. Following close behind was his embarrassed big brother. 'I already *said* sorry to Colin,' he was saying miserably.

But Flora had made a promise and she was going to keep it no matter what. 'Alice, meet Colin,' she said breathlessly. 'Colin, I'd like to introduce you to Alice Midnight, the Afterdark princess.'